UNSPEAKABLE

and Other Stories

UNSPEAKABLE

and Other Stories

LUCY TAYLOR

Lucy Taylor
Pismo Beach, California

Cover design by Joan Iaconetti

ISBN: 978-0-9852399-7-8

Published by:
Lucy Taylor
Pismo Beach, California
http://www.lucytaylor.us/

Printed in the United States of America
Book design by raqoon design

CONTENTS

Introduction

"Home Is Where The Horror Is"

In George Orwell's dystopian novel *1984*, there's a chilling scene where the protagonist Winston Smith is being carted off to the dreaded Room 101, the place where 'the worst thing in the world' awaits. In Winston's case, this 'worst thing' is rats—specifically, starving ones that are going to devour his face. One look at the famished rodents and Winston is begging his captors to spare him and subject his lover Julia to the torture instead.

Most of us have our personal 'worst thing in the world'—a deeply rooted, not necessarily rational fear that trumps all others. Especially when we're alone, in the wolfen hours of the night, the mind veers toward its personal abyss, peeking over the edge with dread and fascination.

I don't know if George Orwell himself had a particular fear of rats, but I do know that writers often use their craft as a way to unearth, explore and sometimes exorcize that which terrifies them. Call it a do-it-yourself form of therapy, a way to shine the light of imagination into the dark and cobwebby corners of the psyche. And if readers are entertained or intrigued along the way, then that's icing on the proverbial cadaver.

When I looked at the stories in this collection, one thing was immediately clear—in the world of my imagination, it's DNA that does us in. Family will get you, be it blood kin or the madhouse that we marry into. Never mind the smiling young Republican who moonlights as a serial killer, the recently axed Wall Street trader armed with a grudge and a Walther 9mm semi-automatic, or the sadistic stranger on the subway who sees in you a dead ringer (pun intended) for the mother or lover who rejected her or him—forget those paltry perils, it's those whose beds or family tree we share (or both!) who pose the gravest menace.

These are the people who share our lives, our liquor cabinets, our debit cards and medicine chests.

They're the ones who know not only where we stash the carving knives but where to stick and how to twist them.

It's these folks, the deranged and delusional members of Families Gone Mad, that I feel compelled to write about, whether or not they were actually part of my personal storyline—drunken and abusive fathers (my own father, a steely and teetotaling Ice Prince was merely absent), demon lovers (I've had one or two), and Cannibal Moms, who see their offspring as an extension of the self they essentially despise.

I write about loved ones who are anything but loving, about families more like a small, private insane asylum than the nurturing safe haven that a family is supposed to be. These are my 'worst thing in the world.'

And yet…sometimes that 'worst thing' leads to its flip side…and salvation.

Not long ago, I heard a woman at a 12-Step meeting say 'There's family of chance and there's family of choice and I choose to be with my family of choice."

Amen to that, sister.

From both my 'families' I've learned important things.

From my family of chance, I learned what it's like to be alone and unrecognized, to be perceived through the prism of delusion, a lost soul marooned in the belly of bedlam. I learned the beauty and power of language, but also its capacity for subtle perfidy, how it can be used to subvert and distort reality, to sanction cruelty and sugarcoat abuse. I learned that words can be the path to freedom or just another lock on the cage door.

And from my family of choice, I learn on a daily basis about love and loyalty, about burdens shared and intimacies treasured, about forgiveness and atonement and joy. I learn about the gift of a difficult childhood and the fact that "it's never too late to have a happy one."

As you'll see, the stories in this collection have a decidedly dark edge, and most of them involve twisted family relationships.

Read them and, if nothing strikes a chord of resonance, be grateful.

If something seems disturbingly familiar, don't despair—we all still have the option of that saving grace—the family of choice.

Unspeakable

Never underestimate the power of words, Christine, my stepfather, Dr. Peyton Eads, used to say. *We think they're only symbols, only sounds, but the right word is like a rare perfume—it has the power to evoke the feelings and sensations from the past and make them real again.*

I was just a kid then. I didn't know what he meant, only that Dr. Eads was a renowned psychiatrist and unquestionably the best of the various "uncles" and boyfriends who had preceded him through the revolving door to Mother's bedroom. But that was because he hadn't yet started to "train" me. Later on, I learned only too well what he meant about the power of words.

Ricky Calloway, as I was to find out years later, understood the power of words as well or better than Dr. Eads and demonstrated that knowledge more dramatically. Unlike in the case of my stepfather, though, I knew Ricky was dangerous and crazy from the start.

It had been over a year since I'd last seen Ricky Calloway when I came home one night to find the lock on my apartment door jimmied and Ricky sitting in my living room, naked, in the dark.

I knew it was Ricky by the bulk of his outline, backlit against the aquarium green glow from the computer screen that threw the only light in the room—his sheer heft was unmistakable, his nudity—when viewed in silhouette—was shockingly apparent. His only concession to clothing was the biker bandanna holding back the mass of black hair that slid over his shoulders like an Apache warrior's.

The first question that popped into my mind—*did you do it?*—was the one I was afraid to ask. So instead I said, "Jesus, what are you doing here? Why'd you break into my place?"

"I didn't know what time you got off work, and I didn't want to wait out in the hall. Don't worry, I'll fix the door before I go."

"Damn right you will. And you'll get dressed."

"When I leave. But maybe you won't want me to leave. Maybe you'll want me to stay the night. I've got something to show you that might change things for us."

Us. What us?.

"What could you show me that could change anything?" I said. "I can't be with you. I can't be with anybody. We tried that once, remember?"

"Well, let's try again," said Ricky. He held a big hand out to me. "Come over here and touch my cock."

"Do *what*!"

I knew Ricky Calloway was a little nuts and I knew I should be afraid of him, but I wasn't. If he'd come back to kill me or extort money, I figured so fucking be it. Considering what I'd set in motion, maybe I deserved it. On the other hand, I knew Ricky was once in love with me, so maybe he still was. Or maybe he just wanted to get laid and figured that I owed him. Big time.

"Christine," he said, "did you hear me?"

"Yeah, I heard you." I sidled into the room and sat across from him on the couch, looking him up and down, trying to assess the extent of his dangerousness. "Give me a minute. I need to think about this."

§ § §

I first laid eyes on Ricky Calloway at my brother Andrew's funeral. Andrew committed suicide two years ago by hurling himself off the roof of the ten-story apartment building where he owned a condo. He didn't jump feet first, which I was told by the police—who tend to know about such things—is the norm, but dived head first, like a Mexican cliffdiver—an aberration even for an act that is itself an aberration.

The funeral was modestly attended, the priest drafted for the occasion a tufted-haired old Benedictine from St. Paul's, the Church that Mother used to attend before her gait grew too tipsily unsteady to make it up the broad pink marble steps. My sister Anne and her husband Robert were there and Andrew's colleagues from the legal firm where he'd worked as a criminal defense attorney. Our younger brother Barnett, the baby of the family and a little slow in the head, came to eulogize his elder sibling and did so with such fervor and at such length that the priest's head drooped upon his chest and snores emanated from his ribby torso.

"Whatever the magnitude of his sin, *God* loves Andrew," Barnett yelled, fist raised as though challenging anyone to argue the point. "*God* has saved Andrew, and he is sitting at the feet of our most merciful *God* and his son, our Lord and Savior *Jesus Christ*."

I'd never heard Barnett rant like this, churning himself into a such a spiritual lather that his listeners were either appalled or simply agog at the display. Barnett shook sweat from his hair like a wet spaniel and rolled his eyes and trembled each time he invoked the name of the Lord. At a certain point, his ferocity began to make me uneasy and I searched for distraction by looking at the reactions to my surviving brother's diatribe in the faces of the predominantly well-groomed and tastefully attired mourners who had made up Andrew's social set.

A couple of people, who didn't fit in any better than Barnett did, caught my eye.

"Who's that?" I said to Anne, indicating the hulking biker type whose glaring black eyes would have been scary if not for his copious weeping.

"That's Ricky Calloway," she said. "When he was sixteen-years-old, he caught his father raping his ten-year-old sister and he stabbed him to death."

I absorbed this, then said, "How'd he know Andrew?"

"Andrew defended him on an assault charge a few years back and they got to be buds. Stop staring at him, Christine, he's a career criminal. Not your type. Even if you haven't been with a man in ten years," she added, squeezing my hand to show she wasn't trying to be nasty, just acknowledging what she viewed as my bizarre and stubborn celibacy.

"Make that fifteen," I said.

Chastised, though, I stopped sneaking peaks at Ricky Calloway and turned my attention to the other person who looked out of place here—the one I figured this Calloway guy would probably end up going home with—a short, zoftig woman whose brassy blonde curls stood out like yellow neon and whose dangly, mini-chandelier earrings twisted in the breeze like tiny hanged men. She must have felt my eyes on her, because she turned suddenly, looking directly at me. Her hand came up in a tiny wave, fingers only, as one waves to a child.

After the service, as everyone drifted back to their cars, the blonde came stumblingly up the hill behind me. She wore a long black skirt slit to the thigh and a grey sweater unbuttoned to allow a glimpse of a pink lace bra. She was easily twice the age I'd originally guessed—blonde hair framing a course, fatigue-lined face, her limbs stocky and muscular—factory worker limbs, well-larded but at the same time powerful.

Then, closer still, I reassessed that thought—not a factory worker at all, but in a matter of speaking, still assembly line. She reeked of brandy and her steel-grey eyes looked slightly out of focus from a lifetime of seeing selectively.

"I'm Katrina," she gushed, forcing a sloppy hug on me. "Andrew and I were close friends, *very* close." She dabbed at her dry eyes to show sincerity. "You're his sister, right?"

"I'm Christine. He mentioned me?"

"Yes, well, not exactly. Not really, no. He wasn't a big talker, Andrew. He more liked me to talk."

She gave a crafty sideways glance. "He left a few things at my apartment, some clothes and a few books, and you know, some other items, items of a sex'shul nature."

"Whatever things you have of Andrew's, I don't want them," I said. "The only thing I'd appreciate, if you have it, is information. Why would he do something like this?"

Her eyeballs rattled around in their sockets as though she'd taken a blow to the chin. "He had a lot of secrets," she managed finally, "but, like I said, he wasn't much of a talker."

I turned and strode away from the stench of her hundred proof breath. I have nothing against hookers, but I'm intolerant of drunks. My mother having been one.

"Hey, wait!" she called.

Incredibly, she was grinning as she staggered after me. "Look, Christine, I liked Andrew a bunch and I got only respect for the dead, whatever way they go, but I have to ask, I gotta know—" She ran a pink pointed tongue along vermillion lips and whispered slyly, "I mean, I thought maybe you could tell me, what does— what did—there were some words he made me say over and over every time we were, you know, intimate—it was the only way he could get it up—but they weren't sex words. They weren't dirty. I wondered, maybe you could, you know, like satisfy my curiosity, what did they—"

"Stop it, I don't want to know."

But she was drunk and one thing I learned from my mother was that drunks neither see nor listen nor care, so she told me anyway. Three words—my brother Andrew's dirty little secrets. They weren't the same Words given me, but I damn well knew where they'd come from and how they'd gotten hardwired into his brain. Just realizing this brought up such rage in me that for an instant I stood looking around for Ricky Calloway, patricidal son, no longer feeling shy or grief-stricken but ballsy and sexy and hot on the make.

I wanted something from Ricky Calloway.

Thank God, when I spotted him, he was roaring away on a Harley, and I watched him go, imagining what kind of knife he might have used to stab his father, how it must have felt when he muscled in the blade.

§ § §

At night, I dream Words. Not Andrew's words. Mine. The consonants whisper against my clit like the stroke of a feather, the vowels ooze wetly like a seeking tongue. I chant them in my mind, these Words that I never say aloud, that no one else has ever heard me utter except the one who first inflicted them upon me.

"Say them, Christine, pronounce them slowly, lovingly," says Dr. Eads as his fingers rove and wander. He has long, pale, beautiful hands capable of elegant, almost balletic movements. In my dream his hands flow over me like cool wine. They weave a lurid tapestry across a befouled loom, uniting sounds and synapses, hotwiring lust and potent shame to sounds that, in standard English, are almost pathetically innocuous. A child could say these words and not be scolded. To the world at large, they are just words.

But to me they are Words that suck and stroke, Words that evoke my darkest memories, that set me on fire and immolate me with shame. Magic Words. The Words that accompanied my introduction to sex and to shame and to secrecy.

§ § §

A few weeks after Andrew's funeral, I went over to my sister Anne's to keep her company while her husband Robert was out of town. We were hanging out, eating popcorn and watching TV. I knew she was worried about something, working up to telling me. Finally, she said, "Barnett is giving me the creeps. When he gave that eulogy at Andrew's funeral, it seemed to have an effect on him."

"What do you mean?"

"I heard he's been going to the Cathedral, preaching sermons, ranting and raving, God-this and Jesus-that. The priests are being good-natured about it—they like Barnett—but it's got to stop. He's interfering with the Masses."

"You want me to talk to him?"

"Would you?"

"No."

We both laughed. "That's what I thought."

We talked some more, Anne trying to persuade me to pay a visit to Barnett, me coming up with reasons not to. Barnett and I are ten years apart in age and miles apart in temperament and lifestyle. "He's eccentric," I said to my sister. "It's why he can't hold down a job. This preaching thing, it's just a phase."

The sitcom we were watching ended and a trailer for a new movie came on, something about the flood of the decade in a small northwestern town. *Hundreds in danger of drowning*, a grim-faced actor was saying to a panicky crowd.

Anne started to giggle, stifled it and stuffed some popcorn into her mouth, almost choking in the process and then spitting it back out into her hand.

I turned to look at her. "What's so funny?"

The giggles pealed out of her like a wildly rung bell.

"Anne, you okay?"

Anne clamped her thighs together and doubled over as the TV voice went on, "*Water surging! A town inundated...*" The giggling wasn't giggling anymore. It had transformed into something else, a jagged, helpless laughter with as much gaiety as a death rattle. She wrapped both arms around her belly, fighting for breath as the compulsive laughter racked her and hissed, "Where's the goddam remote?"

I tossed it to her.

She must have been trying to hit *mute* or change the channel, but in her flustered state, she increased the volume by mistake. *Floodwaters drown a valley...* boomed the voice.

She lurched to her feet and staggered into the bathroom. When she came out, her hands were trembling, and she couldn't look at me.

"Anne, What's wrong? What just happened?"

"Jesus, it's so embarrassing...why do they let them *talk* like that on TV? How the fuck can they allow it?"

"Allow what?"

"The obscenities! The filthy words! Didn't you—" She covered her face. "Jesus, you have no fucking idea what I'm talking about."

Something cold passed under my heart. "What obscenities?"

"Oh, *you* know." She leaned toward me conspiratorially, body language and tone of voice that of a woman confessing to something torrid, banging her brother-in-law, embezzling funds from the school soccer team. "You know, the potty words in that commercial. Hearing them like that, when I didn't expect it, fuck, I had to go jerk off. My goddamn cunt was throbbing. Why does everyone pretend those words aren't nasty when they *are*?"

"Anne," I said, "when Mom was married to Dr. Eads, she was drinking more than ever, and he'd spend a lot of time with us, each individually, making up for her absence, he'd say. Did he do something to you? Those words that made you laugh, did he link them in your mind to—other things?"

For a second, she looked at me as though I'd just landed from the moon. Then her face drooped like a crone's. "You, too?" she said, her voice barely a whisper. "Oh fuck—he did that weird shit to you, too?"

"And Andrew," I said, "I'm pretty sure."

"I always thought it was just me he played those sick games with, and I was too ashamed to tell anyone. But why the words? If he was into molesting kids, that's one thing, but why did he hook the sex up to words that aren't even sex words, that he probably picked out at random."

"Maybe that was the point. He wanted to see if he could take ordinary words and make them erotically charged—forever—for his victims. He was always talking about the way the brain processes language. I think we were his own private experiment."

Anne folded her thin arms around herself. "The son-of-a-bitch. I always felt so ashamed, so crazy. I mean, just hearing those stupid words sometimes will make me come."

"Do you ever ask Robert to—you know—say them when you're making love?"

"You kidding? I know those really aren't dirty words to anyone but me. I'd feel like an idiot. What about you? Have you ever asked a lover to repeat whatever it was Eads said to you?"

I tried to smile, but the corners of my mouth turned down. "It's been fifteen years, Anne. Does that answer your question?"

Her small freckled hands curled into fists. "It isn't fair. He molested both of us, maybe Andrew, too. We should track him down to wherever he's living now and make him pay."

"I've thought about it," I said, "but I'm afraid to try that. I'm afraid it would come back to haunt me."

§ § §

But God has a sick sense of humor and He proved it by letting me run into Ricky Calloway, in the least likeliest of places for either of us to be—a church. Ricky grew up in the same Irish-Catholic neighborhood that I did and, even though far from devout, he still managed to get to confession and Mass a few times a year. I'd gotten a strange call from the priest who gave the eulogy at Andrew's funeral—apparently Barnett was at the Cathedral delivering a sermon. He'd commandeered the church steps and was giving some sort of extemporaneous rant. *Could I please come get him*, the old priest pleaded.

By the time I got there, Barnett was gone, and I was nearly knocked down the pink marble stairs by a huge man with angry black eyes who came barreling through the door. Later, Ricky would tell me that he'd forgotten to put the safety lock on his Harley and had bolted out in the middle of Mass, afraid hoodlums would be making off with his prized bike. He knew how easily and profitably such a theft could be accomplished because it was one of the ways he supplemented his own income.

"Watch where you're going," I snapped.

"I *was* watching," he said, stopping to look me up and down the way he might appraise a communion goblet he was getting ready to filch. "I saw you at Andrew's funeral. You're his sister."

"Christine," I said. "I remember you, too. You're Ricky Calloway." Astonished at my own boldness, I added, "You headed anywhere in particular?"

He grinned. "Straight to hell, according to Father Mark."

"Me, too."

He looked me over again. "That's kind'a hard to believe."

"You'd be surprised."

"Surprise me."

I did—but not, undoubtedly, in the way that he'd been hoping.

§ § §

Considering that we were both, in our own way, desperate, we observed an unlikely regimen of self-control, postponing sex while we became friends. I hadn't had a lover, male or female, in fifteen years, and Ricky had just broken up with a girlfriend and hadn't been with a woman in nearly a week—which somehow, for the two of us, approximated the same amount of deprivation. And we had Pasts. His, he liked to boast about. Mine, I preferred to hide. We'd meet for dinner or drinks, catch a movie. I learned his story, not little by little in dribs and drabs, but in large, nearly indigestible chunks of such mayhem, intrigue, and substance abuse that it resembled an action/adventure series. After the stint in juvie for murdering his dad, he'd worked construction and sold drugs on the side, got busted and gone to prison for drug dealing and assault, weathered two divorces, countless break-ups and the death of his mother, survived a gunshot wound to his thigh that almost severed his femoral artery.

We didn't have sex for four months, partly because I was in denial about what I really wanted from Ricky Calloway, partly because I cherished the fantasy that this time, because he was so different, so outside the conventional norms, I would be different, too, the act of sex itself would be different. Not shameful and sordid and embarrassing, but full of raw lust and vigor and sheer animal exuberance.

When I judged that Ricky could be put off no longer and I had to take the risk, we finally lay together in his bed, kissing and caressing. His body was a tapestry of scars from various mishaps and altercations, fistfights and motorcycle accidents and bullet wounds, in addition to a number of lurid tattoos and painful-looking piercings. While in prison, as part of a gang initiation, he'd notched his right shin with a knife—three equally spaced vertical lines—and carved some sort of Celtic-looking symbol into his forearm. He seemed proud of this self-mutilation, as though it marked some sort of rite of passage.

My fingers kept returning to the scars, especially the self-inflicted ones, tracing them over and over.

"What was it like when you killed your father?"

"A rush," he said. "Better than sex. Then later on, I just went numb, spaced it all out. But I was never sorry for what I did. He deserved it."

I knew for sure then that I wanted Ricky Calloway. From the neck up, anyway. Now if I could just convince myself to want the rest of him.

But the moment he started to penetrate me, I froze and my mind seemed to exit my body like a parachutist abandoning a doomed plane. I invoked my Words, saying them in my mind, but in another human being's presence that only caused a paralyzing shame that numbed my limbs and pelvis. It was as if I was afraid that he could hear me thinking, that he would *know*.

He propped himself on his elbows. "What is it, Christine? I do something wrong?"

"No, you're fine. It's just that, I'm so sorry. I can't—"

"Tell me what's wrong."

"It's not your fault."

His face contorted. "It's me, isn't it? Because you're scared of me. I shouldn't have told you all the shit I've done. That stuff turns women off."

"Not necessarily."

"What is it then? I can force my way inside you, but it'll hurt you and probably me, too, and I don't want to do that."

My mouth was as dry as my pussy, the only part of me that lubricated was my eyes.

"Ricky, I'm sorry. I haven't had a lot of practice at this. I think I'd like sex if I could just be good at it."

"Something happened to you to make you afraid of sex. Tell me."

So I did—most of it anyway.

Ricky listened with a mournful expression on his face, then asked, "What happened to this bastard Eads?"

"The marriage to my mother fell apart because of her drinking, and Eads divorced her. The last I heard, he'd gotten a job at a psychiatric hospital back east and moved away. We never heard from him except at Mother's funeral. He sent me a condolence card. On the back he'd handwritten a sonnet that contained the Words. His little joke. I had to leave the viewing to go masturbate."

"Christ, what a bastard," Ricky said. "Where the hell does the son-of-a-bitch live?"

I almost told him that he'd have to track Eads down, that I wasn't really sure where he lived, but something stopped me. Maybe the fact that I really liked Ricky Calloway and didn't want him to risk another prison term in some possibly misguided quest for vengeance on my behalf. Maybe because I'd planned to at least make love with him first.

Or maybe I just wasn't angry enough.

It took a call from Anne the following week to accomplish that. She told me that Barnett had quit his job as a custodian at a local middle school to "preach" full time—on the steps of the library, outside a daycare center, in the rose garden behind City Hall. His spiritual intoxication seemed to be reaching apocalyptic and dangerous new heights.

"I'm afraid for him," said Anne. "When I tried to talk to him myself, well, put it this way, when the priest talks about having a passion for God, I don't think this is what he means."

When I went to Barnett's apartment, I found him sitting in the middle of his living room with three TV sets turned on—each one to the same religious channel. On each screen, a florid faced, pompadoured Huckster-for-Jesus exhorted his audience to let God provide for food and rent and send cash *now*. The TV screens were blurry with handprints, which puzzled me till I remembered that TV preachers often exhort viewers to "pray" with them by touching the screen.

"Cut that nonsense off," I said, perhaps too harshly, for Barnett looked like a mother whose just been told her blessed newborn resembles a toy troll.

"That's God's message, Christine," he said. "Have some respect."

"Bullshit," I said. "What's going on, Barnett? I know you've always been religious, the only one of us who went to Mass, but I never knew you wanted to be a preacher."

"Till Andrew's funeral, I never realized what it feels like to get up in front of a crowd of people and talk about *Jesus* and *God* and the *Holy Spirit*." He put an emphasis upon the words, drew them out across his tongue and licked the final consonants. "I always said those words alone in prayer, never out loud. I never dreamed the thrill that comes from calling out the name of God and God's son Jesus Christ, our Lord and Savior."

A finger of dread wended its way up my spine. "You like to say God's name, don't you, Barnett?"

His mouth stretched wide in a parody of ecstasy.

"The Lord God is my savior, I sure as hell do. It lifts up my spirit."

Not to mention your cock, I thought, to judge from the hard on that had tented up his pants the first time he said the word *God*.

"Tell me something, Barnett. When we were little and Mother was married to Dr. Eads, did he touch you and do things to you? And did he maybe talk about God while he was doing it?"

Barnett scrunched his forehead as though deeply perturbed. "Why do you always call him Dr. Eads? I call him Dad."

"I know you do, Barnett. So tell me, did he?"

"Did he what?"

"Touch you."

"He calls me sometimes, you know."

"He does?"

"At night, real late. He likes to call me up and talk."

"Where does he call from?"

"A pay phone."

"A pay phone where?"

"Near Noah."

"Noah? Like Noah's ark?"

"Yeah, but new."

"New? Newark? Is that where that scumbag lives now, Barnett, Newark, New Jersey?"

"Why do you hate him, Christine? He's a good man. When he calls, we talk about God. He says God must love me a whole lot, because I haven't forgotten anything."

Oh, Barnett, I thought, *you were just a baby. Oh, fuck.*

I went home and called up Ricky Calloway and told him Newark was where he could start looking for Dr. Eads.

§ § §

"Christine," says Ricky, sitting in my darkened living room almost a year later, "come here and touch my cock."

I see his hand move toward the darker shadow of his lap and look away. I want to want him, but the cold is coming over me, climbing my spine like some inner Ice Age, numbing my heart.

He holds out a hand. "Come here."

I shake my head. "It won't be any different than before. Nothing's changed."

"Give it a try. Please, Christine, just once."

So I do. In the bedroom, I cut off all the lights and peel out of my clothes with my eyes shut, as though this means he won't be able to see me. Then I crawl under the covers where Ricky, having nothing to do in the way of undressing, is already waiting for me.

"I found your Dr. Eads," he says and I made sure where I put the body, nobody's gonna find it for another fifty years. But before I used the knife on him, we had a talk." In the dark I feel him smiling. "And then I used the knife on me."

"You what?"

"I had to stay away until I was sure the scars were going to heal up good and raised. I think you'll like the way they feel. I think you'll want to touch me now. I think you'll want me inside you."

"I don't see—"

"I know your words, Christine. I made him tell me."

I move to clamp a hand across his mouth, but he pushes me away.

"Don't worry, I don't need to say them," he says. "They're as much a part of me now as they are of you. Run your hands over me. Feel the scars." He takes my hand and guides it down. "You can start with my dick."

The Family Underwater

It was soon after my fifteenth birthday that I came home from school one day to find that our frame house on the corner of Monument Avenue and Malvern Street had filled up with water all the way to the second-floor ceiling. I don't mean it was *under* water—it was *full* of water, like a toy house that you'd put in the bottom of an aquarium for the guppies to swim through and the bottom suckers to clean. Inside, my mother and my ten-year-old sister Babette floated from room to room like big soft ballerinas doing a *pas de deux* in soggy slow motion.

I stared through the living room window, afraid to open the front door for fear a torrent of water would rush out, depositing a waterlogged Mom and Babette and all our tacky furniture and used clothing from Second Hand Rose in a big sopping heap on the lawn.

So I hung around outside until Dad staggered home, listing side to side like a ship with an unbalanced cargo, sweat stains the size of volleyballs under his arms and that mean glint in his eyes that suggested his reception that evening at The Tramp Lounge had not been worthy of his stature in Tampa's dominant social class, the Fraternal Order of Drunkards, Bullies, and Butt holes.

But I digress, as Ms. Flannahan in English 202 used to say.

In his own sodden state, Dad didn't even notice the condition of the interior of our house, but opened the door and plunged right into a stationary wall of water, while I gaped through the window. The water didn't seem to distract Dad at all from his mission, which, as usual, was to dump shit onto his nearest and dearest. In that respect, we all functioned at one time or another as toilets.

Tonight, Dad's face was red as a clown's carnation, and his mouth hung open like a piranha with a bad overbite. He was flailing his arms about, but it was all taking place in slow motion, and—best of all—there was almost no sound. Oh, I could hear little gurgles that might have been "goddamn bitch" and "lousy fag bartender" but mostly it was just soft, sucky sounds, like a baby's farts, not scary, but almost comical.

Mom scowled and said something that came out of her mouth in a long string of silvery bubbles. It looked like she was puking up pearls or the egg cases of some exotic sea creature.

Then I saw Dad raise his hand and strike Mom alongside the head, but underwater like that, it took about ten seconds for his hand to connect with her jaw, and a good fifteen more for Mom to go down—in slow, graceful silence, her dress floating up high in the water so I could see her blue underpants billowing, her shoulder striking the edge of the coffee table with a muffled, wet *thrump*.

Something tiny and gold, about the size of a corn kernel floated past the window. It took me a minute to realize it was one of Mom's teeth. I took a deep breath, planning to hold it just long enough to drag Mom and Babette out of the house, and I plunged into the submerged living room.

As soon as I entered the water, Dad came at me. His rubbery lips twisted like a riled moray eel, his mouth working but no sound coming out except the glug-glug of bubbles that sounded like the toilet tank when it backs up. He grabbed for me, but before he could hit me, Babette floated by, breast stroking like crazy, and her red hair fanning out around her head like a halo of flame. She made a shooshing gesture with one finger, and then clasped my hand in a motion so graceful and serene, you'd never have guessed the desperation behind it, and floated up the stairs ahead of me like a drowned angel.

It wasn't until we swam into our room and hid in the closet, hovering up level with the coat hangers that I realized I'd been breathing all along. The water was thick and cold and cloying, like breathing snot, and it took some getting used to, but after a while I didn't notice anymore. I was just grateful for the bizarre fact that I was able to breathe at all.

Those first few weeks adjusting to life underwater were difficult. I slept a lot and had strange, murky dreams in which I drowned and revived and drowned again, but I also began to feel a new and welcome calm, a safe-feeling numbness as if a dentist doing a root canal had missed my gum and shot the novocaine directly into my brain. Cotton candy La-La Land, safe and soft and cushiony, where even the most violent fights erupted in silence and serenity, and blood spilling from my lip or Mom's nose unfurled like gorgeous underwater snakes that slowly dissipated into the pale layers of cornflower blue water. Dad's yelling didn't frighten me, and physical pain, what I felt of it at all, seemed to take place in someone else's body, the sensations distant, like the echo of a train disappearing far down a long tunnel.

I began to regret all those years I'd spent living in the air.

At night, Babette and I would lie together in our submerged bed and whisper back and forth, her bubbles breaking on my nose and mouth like kisses.

"How do you suppose it happened?" I said. "I mean, this isn't possible. For one thing, our house never even kept out a good hard rain—how can it hold in all this water without any of it leaking out?"

"What are you talking about?" said Babette. "Our house has always been full of water. Ever since I was three years old. Don't you remember? It filled up with water the day of Grandma's funeral. Dad got drunk and fell against the coffin, and Mom started screaming at him, and Dad smacked her in the face. When we got home, the house was full of water. I wondered why you never said anything about it."

"Is that why I've never seen you cry? You've been underwater all these years?"

Babette nodded. "I'm sorry. I should have told you. I really thought you were just pretending not to know."

"But that still doesn't explain how it happened. How a house can just fill up with water all by itself."

"Because we need it to be full of water," Babette said. "So we can live here without going crazy."

If there was a down side to living in a house full of water, it was that, after a while I got used to it. To the silence, the slowness, to swimming or floating from room to room instead of walking. Then, *bam*, it was time to go to school or to church or to the grocery store, and the outside world, full of noise and hard edges and sharp, prickly people would hit me like a brick in the teeth, and all I wanted was to dive back underwater.

What was weird, too, was when someone from outside came over to our house, and there I was, safe under the water, but the visitor wasn't, so we'd be moving in two different worlds, a creature of the land and a creature of the sea, hopelessly miscommunicating. After a while I realized that, except for Mom and Babette, it was easier to just be alone.

I remember one disaster that happened right around my first underwater Thanksgiving. I let this boy I liked, Luke Marshak, come over to watch a video. I knew it was a mistake, but Mom had been nagging me to have my friends over, so I did it to appease her. So right in the middle of *Twilight*, Dad burst in, floated into the coat rack and knocked it flat, then did a kind of underwater imitation of an airplane with only one engine trying to take off. A glass lamp got elbowed and shattered in silence, stained-glass shards floating up toward the ceiling, gorgeous as a splintered rainbow, and a tiny fleck of that rainbow nicked Luke above the eye. Drops of crimson floated out of his forehead and stained the water as Dad skidded and went down with a big muffled *flump* onto the floor.

I was so used to this by now, I hardly noticed, but Luke turned the color of skim milk and ran outside like a skinny monkey hopped up on speed. All I could think was what a nerd he was to jump around like that when all he had to do was lie back and float.

I thought I had adapted pretty well to my underwater world until the day Dad ate Babette. Mom was upstairs floating around in the attic, doing the spring cleaning. Dad was downstairs watching mixed martial arts on ESPN, well on his way to replacing all the blood in his body with beer. I was on the computer upstairs, floating happily, doing an occasional slow-motion somersault while updating my Facebook page.

Suddenly Babette gave a screech that was sharp and terrifying even underwater. I swam downstairs in time to see Dad on the floor with Babette pinned underneath him. The water around the bottom of her shorts was turning red. She squirmed away, but Dad caught onto her ankles.

Babette began to swim, swimming and screaming, when suddenly Dad's body stiffened and darkened and elongated. Fins sprouted from his spine and belly, and he became a shark, a great white shark with hideous metallic-colored jaws and eyes that looked like they'd been plucked from a deep-frozen corpse. He opened his mouth and sucked Babette in. He gulped her feet and legs down his throat, then her waist, then her just-budding breasts. The water in the living room churned scarlet. Morsels of what looked like albacore tuna, but that had to be flesh, floated past my face. I couldn't think, couldn't fight, couldn't swim, and Babette's skull was being crushed like an empty beer can—I saw her eyes, glassy and huge, full of terror as her face slid down into his maw, and then our Father the Great White Shark looked toward me and focused on me his unspeakable hunger, that gluttonous urge to devour and destroy.

Without hesitating a moment, I opened a window, took a deep breath, swam outside into the air and—

—fell into the zinnia border and the bright, loud outside world of sharp edges and noise, where I couldn't swim anymore, so I got to my feet and I ran, I ran for my life.

§ § §

A funny thing about how you change when you've lived under-water. The world of light and air never feels right, never quite works. It's like being E.T. for the rest of your life, always searching for a home you can't quite remember and aren't sure you even liked, but the only place that ever felt "normal."

I spent quite a few years in the air world. I hitch-hiked to Phoenix, moved into a shelter for runaway kids, finished high school, and got a job selling ads for a radio station. With a little effort, I learned not to blow bubbles or try to breast stroke across a room, because people would look at me funny. After a while, you'd never have thought I grew up in any place but the air.

Then one evening, coming home after work, I saw a blond boy with a cigarette and a smirk leaning up against the laundromat on the corner. Hard raptor eyes, a ripe, bitable mouth with just a faint trace of cruelty at the corners, a lump in his Levi's that made my heart melt down all slick and hot and wet into my underpants.

I went home with him.

I wasn't disappointed.

His name was Darius. His apartment was a walk-up on the third floor above a liquor store. The apartment was underwater. He opened the door and swam inside. I swam in behind him. We fucked like fish, in silence and cold-blooded splendor, while the water protected us, kept us separate, a buffer through which hate and fear and violence barely registered. Where blood was beautiful and pain an interesting diversion.

I knew I had come home.

A Hairy Chest, A Big Dick, And A Harley

Bethany turns forty-four on Friday, but LizAnn and I decided it'd be best if we went ahead and stopped by with her presents tonight. She'll be freaked out a little bit, 'cause she's not sure when Frank's coming home from his hunting trip, and Frank don't have much use for either LizAnn or me—thinks we're a bad influence on the little wifey—well, he's right, we sure as hell are! We three been friends since third grade and LizAnn and I've been trying to talk Bethany into leaving that scumsucking son-of-a-bitch since the first time he hauled off and whacked her.

LizAnn offered to help wrap the gifts, but by the time we got back from our stay at the lake, she looked, frankly, like she'd been ridden hard and put away wet, to quote an old West Texas girlfriend of mine, and I told her to go on home, take a hot bath with some of that white musk oil she loves, have a good swig of Scotch and get some sleep. I'd wrap up the gifts and swing by in a few hours, and we'd both go over to Bethany's house.

I wouldn't be a bit surprised, though, if LizAnn sleeps right through 'till morning. LizAnn uses sleep the way some women use sex and other women use chocolate. When we were kids, I remember being over at her house when LizAnn's mom and dad were goin' at each other's throats like hyenas, and LizAnn would fall fast asleep on the sofa. She said sleep was the only way she knew to escape.

So I s'pect LizAnn may just sleep a good ten or twelve hours. Which means I gotta wrap up the gifts by myself. That's okay, though, since t'was me kind of started this thing a few years back, when I had just given old Charley his walking papers and LizAnn and Bethany and I were sitting around Bethany's kitchen table (Frank was off on another one of his "hunting trips"—pussy-hunting, that is), and we got to talking about the kind of men we wished we'd married instead of the kind we did, and it turned into this little game, that seemed real innocent at the time, though I guess it ended being anything but.

The idea was to pick three things we'd like in a man that we didn't get in our current husbands or lovers, in other words some "quality, attribute, or possession" as LizAnn says—I'm not kidding, she rattles off words like a talk show host, that gal could emcee *The View*—for which we would happily trade in our present mate.

Well, like I was saying, this was a while back when I was still married to Charley and LizAnn's second husband had just gone to prison for armed robbery and Bethany had tried taking the kids and leaving Frank a couple of times and damn near got killed for her trouble.

So we didn't none of us have a whole lot left to live for except fantasy.

"What three things would you want in a man, Gigi?" Bethany asked.

I didn't have to give it much thought at all, 'cause only a few nights before, I'd taken a hard look at Charley when he was sitting there at his desk, little round executive face all scrunched up over something the NASDAQ had done that day, all earnest and serious and fiscally fit with his flabby white body still decked out in the Brooks Brothers suit he'd worn home from work and I'd known—with the blinding clarity of a screaming white, 10-on-the-Richter scale orgasm—that I didn't care didly for how much money Charley brought home or the fact that every year he studied *Consumer Report* and picked out a vehicle so safe the crash test dummies fight for the privilege of riding in it. At that moment, I knew Charley was history and my destiny, sexually speaking, that is, hung between a different and more muscular pair of legs.

When I said what I'd like my next mate to have, all three of us just rolled on the floor laughing.

So on my birthday, here come Bethany and LizAnn with three beautifully wrapped gifts. One of 'em's an action figure of some WWE wrestling hunk—in real life, the guy's waxed smoother than a pear, but Bethany had cut up a Brillo pad and glued it to the doll's chest. In the next box was a flame red rubber dildo that I swear you could use to plug up a leak in the

Hoover Dam and in the last one, a miniature replica of a Harley XL 1200C Sportster.

Best birthday I ever had and, as LizAnn remarked later on, "a portent of things to come."

Now for Bethany, the first gift we got is this kind'a goofy-looking Dilbert Doll. T'was LizAnn's idea—I wasn't near as creative. What I'd had in mind to do was go over to the Science Museum and get one of them replicas of the human brain that you buy for your teen-agers in the hope if they get a life-like plastic one to take apart, it may stop them from dissecting a real one.

LizAnn, she says I'm probably the only person in the world never heard of Dilbert, this cartoon guy with the funny-looking tie who ain't much with the women, but seems overendowed in the IQ department. So we go to the toy store where LizAnn shops for her daughter Cindi and find this stuffed Dilbert in a cute little suit and striped tie that kind'a reminded me of Charley back when we were still hitched, and that was the gift to represent "brains", which was the first wish on Bethany's list.

So I just got old Dilbert boxed and wrapped, and I'm trying to tie the damn ribbon—my hands are shaking like it's the middle of winter when, in fact, it's damn near ninety degrees outside—when the phone rings, and I snatch at it, thinking it must be LizAnn, maybe having a nightmare or something.

"Gigi?"

Fuck. It's Bethany, all hoarse and scared-sounding, like when Frank's been on a bender and knocked her around.

"Yeah, hon?" I try to sound matter-of-fact, like she caught me in the middle of making a pie crust.

"I need to talk."

"What's up?"

"Gigi, tell me the God's truth. Were you with LizAnn last night?"

"Honest to God, yes, I was."

"Where'd the two of you go?"

"You know LizAnn's got that place up at the lake belonged to her first husband."

"The one robbed the convenience store?"

"No, hon, that was the second one. The first one only did white collar crime, shuffled the deck a few times too many with the company credit cards."

"Oh, yeah, right. So you were with her the whole time?"

"Yes, I was, I swear it."

Bethany draws a deep breath, probably debating whether or not to believe me, I guess, and says, "Well, shit, you could've asked me to go along, too. LeRoy's at summer camp, and Darlene's spending the week with her grandmother, and Frank said he'd be gone all weekend."

"We wanted to invite you, hon, but you know how Frank thinks LizAnn and I are some kind'a feminist/satanist/lesbian posse trying to recruit you to our pussy-licking ways. We didn't want you getting no black eye or broke jaw on account of our little getaway."

"Yeah, you're prob'ly right."

But she must still feel left out, 'cause she starts to cry, big lung-crunching sobs that make my heart hurt.

"What is it, suguh? What's wrong?"

"It's Frank. I think he's having an affair. He left here in such a mad rush Saturday morning, he forgot to take his hunting rifle with him."

"Tell me the truth, Bethany, would you really give a shit if the asshole was sleeping around?"

A long pause. "Yes." Then: "When he has these affairs, they always blow up in his face—then he takes it out on me and the kids."

"That sucks, all right."

"When I couldn't get either you or LizAnn on the phone—well, I know you're seein' that biker guy, but LizAnn, she's having what she calls a dry spell and I thought—I just felt in my bones maybe it was LizAnn off someplace with Frank."

I have to bite my tongue, so I don't burst out laughing, the idea is so fucking ludicrous. Like LizAnn would have that brain-dead redneck dickhead on a diamond-encrusted serving dish with a winning lottery ticket taped to his balls.

"LizAnn screwing Frank? I don't think so, honey."

Now me, I'm ashamed to tell you I'm not as smart as LizAnn and, though I'd never tell Bethany this, I had a little fling with the Frankster once eight or nine years ago. I was bored senseless with Charley, and besides I boozed it up quite a bit in those days. With a half dozen Jim Beams under my belt, Frank didn't look half bad. I realized right quick, though, this was one scary dude, but wouldn't you know it, Frank thought I was hot stuff, and the bastard's been begging me to put my legs in the air ever since.

He also mentioned, by the way, that if I ever told Bethany he'd come back and kill me, and I knew damn well that he meant it.

"I guess I'm bein' silly," says Bethany. "I'm turnin' forty-four in just a couple of days—maybe you and LizAnn forgot—and I guess it makes me feel—"

"Old as fucking Methuselah?"

"That, too. But I was gonna say it makes me feel hopeless. Like I've run out of time, run out of choices. Like nothin's ever gonna get any better."

"Know what, Bethany, I'd love to discuss this, but I'm kind'a in the middle of something."

"Okay, I'll let you go."

"Bye."

Hell, after that conversation now my hands really *are* shaking like castinets. God, I wish I was like LizAnn. Wish I could just fucking *sleep*.

But I can't—I doubt if I sleep for a week—and somebody's gotta wrap Bethany's presents.

Okay, Dilbert's done. Now for the second thing on Bethany's list, which was a sense of humor. Actually we got three things for that: a Comedy Central clip on DVD about a future full of alcoholic robots, a copy of the *SpongeBob SquarePants Joke Book*, and a little naked guy with a key in his back that you wind up and he hops around, pumping his hard-one (LizAnn had her doubts about this one, but I think it's hysterical.)

Now LizAnn, she's always been the serious one of the three of us. It was her idea back when we were all kids that we should pledge eternal friendship. Because women should stick together, she said, and LizAnn ought to know, 'cause she learned the hard way—her Dad run off with her Mom's backstabbing sister when she was twelve.

For someone smart as LizAnn is, though, she's sure had her share of losers. Seems she has something called a "affinity"—LizAnn's word—for men of "grave financial indiscretion and criminal persuasion." Which might not be so bad in and of itself, 'cept LizAnn's men all get caught. She's got two ex's in the State Penitentiary and her last boyfriend's doing six months in the County Jail for felony stalking. LizAnn was so scared, she went out and bought a Colt .45 and got real good at shootin' it, too, just in case Felony Stalker goes back to his old ways when he gets out of the can.

Anyway, that night when we was playing the game, LizAnn told us she wanted her next man to be romantic, law-abiding and loyal.

Well, Bethany and I went out and got her a life-sized poster of that French guy Fabio (not my idea of a *man*, 'less I was a man myself, but that's LizAnn's taste), a sheriff's badge and a toy pistol, and the sweetest little beagle puppy that she adores to this day and who has proved—unlike the ex-husband she named him for—to be utterly faithful.

Okay, back to wrapping Bethany's gifts.

Damn, the goddamned phone again! Oh, don't let it be Bethany. But if it is and if I don't answer, she just might start calling LizAnn, and she's like a kid when you wake her out of a sound sleep, she might just lose it if she hears Bethany's voice.

So I pick up the phone.

"Gigi, I gotta ask one more thing."

"Yeah, honey? What is it?"

"Did LizAnn by any chance tell you that awful lie about Frank?"

"What lie would that be, sweetie?"

"Did she tell you or not?"

"How would I know if you don't say what it is?"

"Then she *did* tell you?"

"Good Lord, Bethany, she did tell me something about—"

"Cindi?"

"I'm afraid so. That day LizAnn and Cindi stopped by and you and LizAnn went upstairs for a minute to have a little nip, just the two of you, and Frank and Cindi were alone a few minutes. Yeah, she told me."

"It's not true."

"The hell it's not. You know he's dangerous, Bethany. It's one thing if he beats you and you take it, but when he starts in on your own friend's daughter—"

"Gigi, he says Cindi's *his*!"

"He's a liar, Bethany, you know that."

"Is she?"

"Well, if she *was* his, which she isn't, does that make it all right for him to put his hand up her skirt? That keepin' it in the family stuff's okay with you?"

"He didn't molest her."

"Jesus, Bethany, how do you know? He beats the shit out of you. Why wouldn't he molest little girls?"

She starts sobbing. "I just wish he'd come home. But I'm scared when he *does* come home, he's gonna be mad about something and—you know, take it out on me and the kids."

I try to make my voice soft and kind, but I've run out of compassion where this situation's concerned. Bethany ought to have done something about Frank a long time ago. Somebody ought to have done something. "Bethany, you know you ought to have left him."

"I've tried, Gigi. You know I have. If I leave him, he'll just track me down again like he did before, and he'll kill me this time. He'll kill the kids. Oh, God, I just wish—"

"What, Bethany?"

"I wish we could go back and be kids again. Make new choices. I wanted somebody strong. Somebody who'd take care of me. What I got was—"

"—a fucking nutcase."

"A control freak."

"A coward and a sadist."

"A cold-hearted man."

No shit.

"Bethany?"

"What?"

"I know you're upset and I don't like to be rude, but I *really* have to hang up now."

"Maybe I'll call LizAnn, see does she have time to talk."

"I wouldn't right now. She's real wore out from the trip."

"It still hurts you didn't ask me to go."

"Honey, trust me, we had your best interests in mind. I gotta go now. Hang in there. Okay?"

Well, damn, that was fucking uncomfortable. She calls again, I won't answer the phone. I don't care if she does wake up LizAnn.

Now where the hell did I put—? Oh, yeah. Over here.

Shit, this is the tough one, but once this last gift gets wrapped, I can shoot right on over to Bethany's house. I won't even bother LizAnn—she's scared of the water, so going out on that lake in a teeny little rowboat in the middle of the night really wiped her out, let me tell you.

Now a heart, I guess I always knew they don't look like no Valentine heart, all cherry red and symmetrical and pointy-tipped, but I didn't realize they're all squishy and maroon-colored and disgusting, till we cut Frank's out of his chest before dumpin' him into that lake.

Getting Frank to meet me out at LizAnn's cabin, though, wasn't no problem at all after I told him how I dream about his cum squirting all over my titties—only thing squirted was Frank's brains when LizAnn stepped out from behind the wardrobe and blew open his skull with that Colt.

A man with a heart, that was Bethany's third wish, but then she added something else, and that part's got me stumped, I must admit.

'Cause how the hell do I keep it warm?

Wall of Words

I burned the Wall of Words last night, right before I headed south on Highway 87 toward Colorado.

It torched just like a big old funeral pyre, and I watched 'til the last ember sizzled and charred and the last vowel crisped and the final consonant became just so much soot.

Pa's famous Wall of Words, the talk of northwest Nebraska, that people came all the way from Denver and Sioux Falls and Kansas City to see, now it's only so much blackened kindling.

No more words.

Just silence, except for the breeze whistling through cinders and ash.

Enough silence now even for Pa, I 'spect.

We never talked much around our house in Hay Springs, Nebraska, mostly 'cause Pa forbid what he called "idle gabbing," that is, conversations that wasn't absolutely necessary.

Myself, I guess I wouldn't have minded a bit more talk, but then Pa took up his carving hobby, and I figured we had words to spare, more words than I ever knew existed: long complicated words like *fornication* and *serendipity* stacked up on the mantel, peculiar words like *quandary* and *abacus* on the coffee table, chunky words like *gash* and *brood* stoppering the doors.

I never did know what most of 'em meant and Pa, he probably didn't either. He just found 'em in the dictionary and liked their shape and sound, figured they'd look right attractive on somebody's dresser top or whatnot shelf.

Pa, you see, was a wordsmith. Not some wuss with nothin' better to do than peck out words on a typewriter or a computer, but a real wordsmith. He *made* words. In the shed back of the house, what I reckon some people would call his studio, Pa carved words out of balsa and pine and cherry and other things besides.

It started soon after Pa came back from prison two years ago, when I'd just started tenth grade for the second time. Pa'd been a champion bull rider and calf roper during the years my older brother Josh and I was little, and he spent the best part of the year on the road. Then he got convicted of attempted murder after knifing a rodeo clown that Pa claimed drove him half crazy singin' Gene Autry tunes all the time. When Pa got out of the joint after six and a half years, that was the end of his career on the rodeo circuit.

I guess maybe he developed a taste for silence in prison, though, 'cause after he come home, Pa started to complain that Ma talked too much. She was a "jabberjaw," as he put it, and Josh weren't much better; Pa called him a "yakkity-yak." Pa forbid Ma to say anything that wasn't absolutely necessary, which I always figured was why she communed with Jim Beam so often and so long. One night, though, after Ma'd threatened to leave Pa the first time some drinkin' buddy offered her a ticket out of town, she screamed, "If words was money, Ben Foley, you'd be the richest man in Nebraska, the way you miser every syllable away!"

Well, that musta' gave Pa an idea. Next day he bought some wood and sharpened up the old carving knife he used for whittlin' back in his rodeo days and he started to carve out words.

At first Pa carved ordinary words — folks' names and a few inspirational words, but he tired of that real quick. He bought a dictionary and browsed in it for longer and more unusual words whose letters lent themselves to squiggles and corkscrews: long words and short ones, adverbs and nouns and adjectives, swear words and sex words (which he always carved small, but with a lot of fancy doodads), even a few foreign words — *Himmel* and *merde* and *Kindertot* are a few I recall.

Pa didn't just carve words, you see, he made works of art. He'd spend all afternoon curlicuing the ends of the "l's" in *languid* and *lewdly* and *longitude* or turning the "b" in *betrothed* into a fire-breathing serpent singeing its own tail.

The more Pa carved, the less he talked and the more he enforced the No Idle Chatter and No Speakin' Unless Spoke To rules. And Ma, she took to drinkin' in nearby towns like Rushville and Chadron, and sometimes didn't come home for days at a time. When she did straggle in, Pa wouldn't say nothin' at all, but from the door of his workshop he'd hurl a word at her — *slut* or *bovine* or *perversity* — as she teetered on up the walk with her hair teased like a bird's nest and her clothes rumpled and soiled.

And Ma'd retaliate by letting loose a stream of words fit to shame the devil himself.

"You daft old bastard, you with your goddamn woodcarving, you got woodshavings for brains! Why can't you *talk* to me, holler or curse, like any normal man?"

But Pa'd just glare and pull his silence round him like a cloak and turn his back to her.

By this time, Pa'd bought a router and an assortment of attachable drill bits and cutters, so he could make his words bigger and more complex. Some of the letters stood two or three feet high, and the shed where Pa worked was so full up with words, the walls looked like pages out of a dictionary.

Finally, I come in from school one day and saw he'd commenced to building something with the words. At first, I thought it was some kind of sign or joke or pun, but I soon realized the words stacked up in the backyard held no particular significance or sense. *Thimble* and *kissing* and *macaroon* formed part of the base with *slurp* and *bereavement* and a very highly ornamental *clannish* topping these and then some other words, short ones, on the third tier. Pa'd driven nails into the wood to hold the words together. The wall rose maybe four feet high then, at its tallest point, and stretched 'bout ten feet long.

Soon after the wall went up, my older brother Josh, who had a small farm of his own across the highway, stopped by the house one Saturday to ask me would I go with him to talk to Pa about what we referred to as "Ma's past-time."

I agreed to go, but my heart was heavy...havin' a conversation with Pa was about as easy as gettin' milk out of a chicken.

But Josh was always better with words than I was and less afraid of Pa, too, him bein' older and livin' on his own.

"We gotta do somethin' about Ma," Josh said, standing there in the shed while Pa carved. "Get her into a rehab or something."

Pa was working on the tail of the "y" in *chastity*, and he finished it before he replied, which took a good ten minutes.

"A drunk tank?" he said finally.

"No sir, I was thinkin' more like a treatment center."

Pa carved on. Five minutes later, he said, "She's like the lot of y'all. You gab too much, fritter away your time. Jabberjaw and yakkity-yak, all day long."

He blew loose wood shavings off the letters.

"But Pa, I think..."

He looked up, eyes hooded and hawkish, wood-chips clinging to his beard like dark beetles. He stared at me, and I felt just like he'd turned the router on me and was drillin' out parts of my gut.

"How 'bout you, Billie-boy? You gonna have your say, too?"

I couldn't have admitted it then, not even to myself, but I was scared of Pa. He wielded silence like a club, and the few words that he ever spoke were more the kind that separate than those that might make bridges.

"No, Pa, I ain't got nothin' to say."

His eyes carved me up in sections, and I thought about that rodeo clown back in Denver and how many stitches they said it'd took to put his face back together.

"You goin' into town today?"

"Yessir."

He nodded, concentrating on the wood.

"Be long?"

"Few hours mebbe."

"Bring me back some Copenhagen…"

"Yessir."

"…and your Ma some whiskey."

"But Pa…I…"

Pa reached for his dictionary and opened it to choose another word. I peered over his shoulder and saw his long fingers pick out *scrumptious*.

"…about Ma, I think…maybe…"

But he wasn't listening anymore, and I knew if Josh and I stood there all day long, we'd get no discussion from him.

§ § §

Not long after Josh tried to talk to Pa, Ma went out on a drunk, and didn't come back. I figured she'd turn up in a few days, like she always did, but when a week passed, I decided she musta' gone and done it, run off with some man who asked her to, like she'd been threaten' to do ever since Pa took up his carving. I didn't say nothin' about it, not even to Josh. I missed

Ma, but I felt happy that she'd run away. For a while there, I had dreams of me and Ma together, in a fancy party at a big mansion, where everyone talked and laughed about their hopes and dreams and fantasies, and the words just flowed all over each other, all rainbow-colored and glowing like fireworks in the dark.

I hoped wherever she'd run off to there'd be lots of people she could talk to.

Meantime, with Ma gone, Pa worked even harder.

The Wall of Words, as people had begun to call it, was getting higher, longer. Pa added *elephantine* and *gargoyle* and *parsimonious*, carved vertically like totem poles out of huge beams of wood with smaller words connecting them horizontally like in a crossword puzzle. People started taking notice from the road and dropping by to look around, but Pa wouldn't let them inside the shed no longer. He kept it locked, and hardly ever came out at all 'cept to take a piss and nail another word onto the Wall.

Meantime, the visitors that stopped by took pictures of each other by the Wall and let their kids crawl over it 'til finally Pa put up a fence around it and a sign saying DO NOT TOUCH and NO TALKING.

Over the next few weeks, dozens of other words were added, *obsequious* and *foreboding* and *juvenile*, *malcontent* and *kindness* and *adroitly*, and the Wall just kept getting higher and longer, and some letters were as big as fireplugs and others fancied up with vines and buds and scrollwork, and Pa kept addin' to it, sometimes two or three words a day.

Josh stopped by my room one afternoon while I was laying there, having me a little sip of Scotch and daydreaming about Ma and me gossiping together at some fancy party. He was all fidgety and nervous and had that clenched jaw look he gets when he's been grindin' his teeth at night.

I stood up and offered Josh a pull from my bottle, but he just sneered and said, "Now that Ma's run off, you gonna be the family lush?"

"Helps me kick back," I said, which was true. With enough booze in me, I could kinda float in and out of that grand, high society party in the mansion where Ma and I drifted among high class nobility, with Ma chitchatting to her heart's content and me confiding my life story to a beautiful big-bosomed lady in a low-cut red gown like one I saw dancing with Johnny Depp in a pirate movie one time.

"Look, we got to *talk*," Josh said.

That made me uncomfortable. It's one thing to fantasize about something, another thing to do it. Josh knew we didn't talk in our family. That wasn't our way.

I shrugged. "'bout what?"

"The goddamn Wall."

"Yeah?"

"Have you *looked* at it lately? Since Pa put up the fence and started makin' it longer?"

"I glance at it from time to time."

"Some of those words, Billie…"

"Yeah?"

"I think…"

And we stood there, staring at the floor, the windows, everywhere but at each other, 'til I took another swig and lost my balance and plopped back on the bed, and Josh said, "Ya damn drunk...when you can see straight, just go take a look at the Wall."

"Where you goin'?" I said as he walked out the door.

"To talk to Pa," Josh said.

And that was the last I seen of him.

§ § §

After that, it was hard to gauge how many days passed, cause most nights I'd drink and doze off or pass out maybe, and the sun would be comin' up and I'd haul my ass off to school, but like as not I wouldn't go at all. School was a lot like Pa's Wall...just words on top of words that made no sense, all meaningless and stupid.

But when I went by Josh's place sometime later to see would he lend me a few bucks to buy some Wild Turkey and I seen Josh's truck was there but he wasn't anywheres around, I got a little worried. I knocked on the door of Pa's shed to ask if he'd seen Josh anywhere.

Pa unlocked the door and stood there, his big frame blocking my view of everything but one end of his workbench, where the router lay with a particularly vicious-looking cutter slotted into it.

"Josh?" said Pa. "Ain't seen him."

"Not this week?"

"Naw."

"Last?"

"Yep. He stopped by to talk."

This surprised me. "About what?"

Pa actually smiled, but on him it looked unnatural, the muscles at the corners of his mouth hunched up like the hind end of a rutting hound.

"He come by 'cause he got the idea he'd like to sign up with the rodeo for a spell. I give him the names of some buddies of mine he could call up in Laramie and Denver. Told him they could help to get him started. He was all fired up about it. We sat up 'til past midnight with me tellin' him my stories. If he ain't been around of late, I reckon he left to join the circuit. Reckon he'll do right fine, too. Takes after me, Josh does."

And Pa shut the door in my face.

It was the most words I'd ever heard Pa speak all at one time.

It got me to wonderin'.

§ § §

That evening I studied the Wall, looking at the words that had been added since Ma disappeared. There was *mercenary* and *idolater* and *spinnaker*, and below that *flummery* and *euphonious* and dozens of others, words of all shapes and sizes and different materials, and I noticed it then. The two long, light-colored words. Nearly white. Smaller than most and stuck into spaces between the bigger words that were carved out of pinewood and balsa.

There on the side of the Wall, I saw *jabberjaw* and a little ways from that was *yakkity-yak*. They was half hidden by some bigger words, but their paleness made them stand out real sharp.

I musta stared at them two words half an hour or more, running my fingers over each letter, learning their shape and their feel and trying to realize their meaning.

And when I thought I understood, I wrenched loose a word near the top that was carved out of teak, and I went lookin' for Pa.

§ § §

Words. In Mexico, where I'm headed, I'll hear them, but I won't understand. They'll fall over me like so much freezing rain.

And if I start to understand, I'll move on. To Japan or Vietnam maybe, anyplace where the words, to me, are nothin' more than decoration — singsong, meaningless sounds like birdcalls on a hot summer morning.

'Cause I can't go back to Hay Springs, Nebraska, never.

That new length of the Wall, the earth below it had been disturbed, dug up and then repacked before the words were piled on top. And them white words I found — *jabberjaw* and *yakkity-yak* — they was carved from bone.

And Pa? Well, right before I burned the Wall, I cornered him in that shed of his with all the bloodstains on the walls and I killed the silence-loving, murdering old bastard.

With *kindness*, right between the eyes.

Prenuptials

In her dream, the witches bend over her cradle singing a lullaby. The words change, but the meaning is always the same: men are evil and lust-crazed. Fantasies of brute power lurk behind their avuncular smiles. Women exist to be demeaned and defiled and destroyed—the phallus is the sword that a woman falls on when she decides to kill herself.

We tell you about these terrible things only to protect you, coo the witches. *Only because we love you and wish you to come to no harm.*

In another land, the witches might have spread her legs and carved away her clitoris and labia. These hags do their mischief with loving lies and lewd caresses.

But you must never want these men, they croon as they gaze at her—so young and promising, her whole life spread out before her—with eyes made dead by jealousy. *You must never want to be the object of their lust.*

No good girl ever wants this.

And so is laid the curse.

Unspeakable

§ § §

There are good men in the city where she grows up, goes to school, and studies painting. Kind and generous, nurturing men. She meets them/likes them/goes to movies and to dinner with them, but she cannot recognize them as potential mates. For it is not these men that make her moist and swollen as she flies toward them like a heat-seeking missile. These men don't give her nightmares from which she wakes up wet. They don't make her heart brake to a skidding stop and cause her blood to whip and flutter like it's full of tiny electric eels.

It's the men the witches told her she must never want that make her feel like that.

She doesn't realize this is what she's looking for until she finds him.

§ § §

She meets him at a meeting for people like herself who suffer from addiction problems. She never expected to find this *kind* of man at such a meeting. For aren't these men in recovery? Isn't theirs an enlightened masculinity, strong yet sensitive to women's needs? The kind of men that make good friends, but never lovers? She doesn't even permit herself to think of sex when she sits in the meeting rooms—she thinks that would be wrong. She crosses her legs and neuters herself and assumes everyone else does the same.

But from the first words they exchange, there is an uncanny link between them, the kind of instant empathy that, if they were into New Age beliefs, might lead them to conclude they'd shared a previous lifetime. Their eyes lock with a click like handcuffs closing. No bomb squad could defuse such incendiary chemistry. Right away they guess each other's secret song. For a band of witches presided at his cribside, too, only their lullaby was different and their curse was for not only him, but for his future mate: *women want only one thing—to be defiled, debased, destroyed. A woman's submissiveness is the yardstick by which a man measures his phallus.*

But you must never want to do such things, they sang as they caressed his baby penis. *Good boys don't.*

And you must never want this.

And so it is lust at first glance, rivetting and irrevocable and, after a few exchanges, he follows her out to her car.

Eyes her up and down as if she's something shiny in a gem store window and he's about to smash the glass to get to her.

"Do you have any clothes you wouldn't mind having destroyed?" She meets his black ice gaze. "Why?"

"Because I want to rip them off you."

She smiles and shivers, slides into her car.

But the game's begun. The distant noise she hears is the sound of witches howling.

§ § §

A day or two later, their enactment of the curse is well under way. She sprawls in his bed, limbs akimbo, her brain on hold as she gazes at this source of her enchantment. He is hirsute and sinewy, virile and veined. She can barely get all of him down her throat. When she thinks of having him inside her, her pussy grips and pulses like the mouth of a suckling child.

"This doesn't feel like a fling," he says. "I've never wanted anyone so much. I think I'm falling in love with you."

She nods and murmurs that she feels the same, although since meeting him, the night terrors from her childhood have come back. She's seen him dip his cock in poison before he puts it in her mouth.

He pulls her to him, folds her flesh against him like a silky garment. He closes his fist in her hair.

"I'm not letting you go. Understand? I'm never letting you go."

Her body's reaction to this mix of menace and endearment is so intense that it temporarily obliterates the power of thought. Her inner muscles start to clench and unclench; the motion travels to the muscles in her belly, which start to undulate.

It's like giving birth in reverse—she wants to pull him in, possess him as utterly, as wantonly as he now possesses her.

He hovers at her entrance, then plunges in and halts. Like one well-studied in the tantric arts, he stays inside her, hard and motionless.

"Do you line your pussy with silk?"

She does a rippling belly dance upon her back. It's getting hard to know where his skin ends and hers begins. Her brain cooks with heat and pheromones.

"Did you mean it? About never letting me go?"

He doesn't answer, but starts to thrust. What begins as a languid glide accelerates into the stomping/pounding/piledriving frenzy of a mosh pit. Her mind glazes over, but her body was never so alive as she arches up to meet the blows delivered by his hips.

She has her answer.

§ § §

If their nights are dedicated to sensuality, their mornings are monotonously mundane. She has coffee with him in the living room while the morning news is on. He turns pages of the paper and reads snippets of current events to her. She dips her bagel in her coffee. It smells moist and sweet as his sweat. She puts on a tasteful business suit, picks up the alligator briefcase that he suggested she buy.

He kisses her. "Good-bye, gorgeous."

When she looks back, he is standing naked in the doorway with a hard-on. The jut of it snags at her heart. She wants to go back, fall to her knees, pay homage with her mouth. At the same time, she wants to leap out into traffic and let something fast and huge and hard smash her to rubble and get it over with.

"Good-bye sweetie, see you tonight."

§ § §

Since childhood, she has believed that she will never marry or have children. The legal contract, the binding ties, it smacks, she's always thought, of bondage. And as for children, there's this secret fear in her—

she can't say why, but has the deep suspicion that something in her might some day wish to do her children harm.

No, she will be an artist, will work only to support her art—wait tables in Aspen or Redstone or Carbondale—cultivate the friendship of free women like herself, maybe enjoy a lesbian affair or two and pity the humdrum lives of the tourists, couples always, snotty kids in tow, who surely must be envying *her* unfettered artist's life. Her recurrent dreams of rape and domination will be transformed into brilliant canvases of wind-whipped mares and earth goddesses with swollen breasts and thighs as thick as tree trunks.

She will let no man contain her.

But she has forgotten her own Bewitchment and the lush allure of her cradle song.

And she hasn't counted on *him* and how they both get high on escalating the erotic games, making more real and harrowing the fantasy of possessor and possessed.

In the course of a few days, they play with ropes and knives and, most dangerous of all, they play that they're in love, that she will be his wife, and that this will last Forever.

They craft bondage scripts that they act out with her spread-eagled on the bed, bent over the balcony railing, posed bitch-style on all fours before the mirrored wall, and without an ounce of alcohol, she gets drunker and drunker until the room starts spinning, and open is the only posture that she knows.

§ § §

"After we get married," she says, toying with her words as her fingers massage and cup and stroke, "what if we go to a party, and I flirt with another man?"

"Then we'll have to leave," he says coldly.

"Then what?"

"We'll get in the car and drive away. As soon as we're out of sight of the house where we've been visiting, I'll reach over and tear your blouse open and rip open your bra. I'll call you a whore, and I'll drive very fast and you'll be afraid—with good reason."

"I know," she says, shivering closer to his heat, "I'll be very afraid. I'm afraid now."

"Good," He says. He is very hard now. His erection presses against her thigh.

"After we get home," he says, "I'll throw you down across the bed. I'll fuck you till you can't remember that you've ever been with any man but me. I'll make you plead for my forgiveness. I'll make you love me."

She can feel her flesh melting into his, merging with his body, at these images. Her clitoris is pulsing as if it will erupt into flame.

"I already love you," she says. Her sigh sounds like blood seeping out of a wound. "I love you, and I want to marry you."

"Oh, you will." He says it like a death threat, and it is. He kisses her, turns her around and mounts her from behind. He yanks her head back by her hair and puts the other hand across her mouth, riding her wildly and brutally, transforming her into something as bright and beautiful and lifeless as the paintings she no longer paints, suffocating her will down to embers and ash.

§ § §

She has never been sure what he does with his days. For a while, she fancied that he had a secret life, perhaps some enterprise outside the law, perhaps another lover. She almost hoped he did. Now she believes he simply stays at home and naps and watches videos, does a 12-Step meeting now and then, meets friends for tennis. Idleness becomes him. He's like a great, sleek lounging Tom who stirs himself only to yowl and feed and copulate. He's like a force of nature. He need only *be*.

As for her own ambitions, she gave up the idea of Art in Aspen long ago. She lacks the time, the drive, the will. Making art requires energy and freedom, both of which are forfeit to her obsession. So she works at an office job and congratulates herself on her practicality and how well she manages to support them both.

At work, she is a model employee, concise and punctual, dependable. Only now and then, distracted, seeming almost dazed, she makes careless mistakes, receives a reprimand. She always takes it well. She is so prompt, so malleable, so docile.

A few of her co-workers have tried to be friends. She smiles and offers a facsimile of friendship, but in truth she is too ashamed to let them know her as she is, a one-time artist, now merely a part of *him* that goes out into the world, that plays a part. She cannot let them know she is addicted to his flesh, that she is a suicide in progress.

§ § §

"When we get married," she whispers, "I want the ceremony to include the words love, honor, and obey."

"Oh they will," he assures her. He stops fucking her and grinds his cock inside her, grips her wrists. Impaled and pinned, she can feel her mind entering that red trance of sex-bliss, that small death from which she knows that she may not emerge. "You will always obey me. You *must*."

"I want you to own me," she says, hating herself as she says the words. Hating the words. Not knowing where they come from, but hating the self-loathing that inspires them.

Hating *him*.

"I already own you," he says. His dark face hovers above her. He is handsome, almost beautiful, a terrifying angel with black brows and the subdued snarl of the gentleman rapist in his voice.

She feels herself become more willing, more daring as she teeters on the edge of the void. Surely no aerialist ever practiced so thrilling a maneuver on the high wire. She is drunk with danger, half swooning from her sense of self-destruction, her seeming inability to save herself.

"I want to marry you," she says, knowing what she really wants is not to want him. But he is the one that the witches sang about. He is her destiny.

He knows very well what she wants. He is inhumanly hard now. "You are already wed to me," he says. "You are already owned."

She arches against him. She wants to feel the tip of his cock draw blood from her heart. She feels like she is aging in reverse. She is that little girl again that the witches loved as their own and hated as their rival, and every kiss upon her face is poison and every touch re-opens unseen scars. In her folly, she thinks that her lover is healing the wounds, that he is filling her with him.

God, she loves Him.

One night they watch a movie where a woman kills a man to avenge her lover's death. He seems to relish this. Rewinds the tape to watch the scene again.

"Would you kill for me?" he asks.

No.

"Yes, I'd kill for you," she says in that whispery, on-the-edge-of-orgasm voice.

"I don't believe you."

"I *would*."

When she falls asleep with her face pressed to the black pelt of his chest, she is a child again and she is loved—she has only to please him always, do whatever he says—and she will be loved forever.

§ § §

Earning his love is a full-time job. A career choice. A commitment.

She hones her acting skills. She knows he senses the slightest rebellion in her heart, the smallest cache of secrets. He has nothing to do with his days but focus on her, meditate upon each nuance of her speech and body language. Is her love diminishing? Does she talk too much on the phone, take extra minutes getting home? Is she being subtly neglectful of his vast and mounting needs? Is she such a fool that she might plot to leave him?

When he grows bored, he amuses himself by finding fault with her. At other times, he gazes at her with the pride of one who's just retouched a museum masterpiece, brought it back to its former splendor, improved it, and when she questions the intensity of that look, he says, "Just thinking of all the plans I have for the rest of your life."

She had plans, too—once. If she could just remember what they were...

He finds her sketchbook one day, and his derision of her drawings are so surgically adroit that she feels naked as a peeled persimmon. Later, when he sees her tears, he soothes her with his skillful tongue and nurtures her with semen.

§ § §

Sometimes she contemplates his Smith and Wesson as one would study a map of some exotic land. She parts herself with the cool, hard barrel and thinks that she should let the gun become her lover, that this must be the ultimate fuck. Even hotter and harder than *him*.

Nonsense, she tells herself. She can walk away from him when she gets ready. She can quit at any time. She gave up alcohol, didn't she? Almost five years without a buzz. Not counting the high she gets from sucking cocktails from their original container. She knows he isn't good for her—she devours self-help books like bonbons. She'll quit this, too, and get on with her *real* life—it's just that she's not ready.

Yet.

She knows the game is aging her. Grey half-moons smudge her eyes. Her face has a haggard, refugee quality, but her body still throbs in sync with his. The athletic and aesthetic quality of her erotic performance is undulled. She can mimic dying with a hot, uncanny sensuality, as though she's done it many times. In the quiet of the night, she fancies she can hear her soul unraveling.

§ § §

"I want to marry you."

Sometimes she says the words alone, to herself, marveling at how they sound, at the unnaturalness of them. What started as a game, a tease, is becoming real.

Love, honor, and obey.

She loves him not at all and honors him only when she must, but obey she will. She must. For doesn't she deserve to die? She's a bad girl, isn't she? For craving his flesh in her mouth, in her cunt, for aching to eat him like some ripe and rotting fruit, the sweet center spewing into her mouth and seeping down her throat as she bites and sucks and hungers more for having sucked his poison.

"I'd kill for you," she whispers.

She almost means it now. The ledge on which she walks is narrowing. The abyss at the bottom of her lover's eyes croons to her and bids her jump.

Prenuptials

One night he ties her with soft sashes and runs a knife across her flesh. He parts her lips. Tells her, in snuff flick detail, what he could do to her.

He could. He *might*. She's wet just thinking of it.

For doesn't love mean being fed upon, consumed, annihilated in the arms of the beloved? She learned that somewhere long ago. It feels like it's imprinted on her soul, encoded into her very DNA. Carried on her X chromosomes like a gene-linked disease.

He puts his hard-on to her lips, then the knife, then his cock.

"Which one?" he says. For a moment, she can't choose.

The only thing she fears more than him is the thought that she might lose him.

§ § §

On the day that she will marry him, (an elaborate ceremony in the East Coast City where his parents live) she looks into the mirror as if into a crystal ball and sees the future like an evil spell spread out before her. She cannot leave him; she's too far gone. She no longer believes she can exist without him. But as her dependence on him has increased, so has her hatred; she longs to pay him back for what she's let him do to her.

Soon after their wedding, she comes into their bedroom, thinking that she'll let him fuck her one more time, give him a final opportunity to end it before she does.

She finds him fallen asleep with the TV on, hair like black fur against the pillow, thighs parted just enough that she can be tempted by his beauty one more time.

But good girls never want this.

She puts the pistol against his temple, admiring the aristocratic plane of his jaw, the thick black lashes, wondering what it would be like to fuck him with a bullet.

But she wasn't raised like that. She isn't meant to kill this way. No, her killing must be done in increments and secret.

She puts the gun away and comes to bed. The old nightmares threaten her, but she takes solace in his skin.

§ § §

When she gets pregnant, he says he doesn't want the child. A baby will take time away from him—he tells her they'll be happier without one.

For the first time since she's known him, she stands up to him. Her wrath shocks her and frightens him. The power of mother love seems to give her a resolve she's never known. A child, she thinks, will be something to belong to her—to take the place of the life that she will never have. For the first time since she's known him, her life soothes down into a sluggish calm, a kind of tranquil torpor. Finally there is something of her own he cannot take away.

The baby is healthy and beautiful. She names it for her mother, and she loves it with a fierce and cannibal cunning.

But the father is the one seduced and charmed. The child becomes his little sweetheart. He dotes on her and plans for her a future full of independence and achievement.

When the baby is a few months old, she sits beside the crib one night, admiring the beauty of her daughter's face, her laughing eyes and guileless zest. Surely this child will have a charmed life—unlike her cursed one.

The baby frets as she bends over the crib. She has her father's mouth. The mother feels a rush of loss and loathing. How dare *his* daughter look forward to the kind of life that she has forfeited. Black envy seethes inside her.

She searches her mind for a gift appropriate for the daughter of the man that she despises.

And it comes back to her—bitter and seductive, the words like licorice laced with strychnine, dark and sweet and sickening.

The words change, but the meaning is always the same: men are evil and lust-crazed and dangerous... women exist to be debased and defiled...

...but good girls never want this.

You must never want this.

And so the curse is passed.

That night, when she lies down next to her husband, her sleep is deep and dreamless.

Ceilings and Sky

Tonight the Master sucked the blood from a cut I'd opened up on the inside of my thigh. Afterwards, he kissed me with his crimson lips. I felt Reborn.

I am sitting in the back row of a Greyhound bus hurtling through the desert toward Las Vegas, reading over and over the journal that my twenty-two-year-old son Nigel kept in the months before he hanged himself. The journal, along with a few of his effects, was sent to me by one of his ex-lover's, a bearded, raven-haired boy named David whom I know only from a photo of himself and Nigel that he included among the items forwarded to me.

"Nigel and me, in better days," he'd scribbled on the back. "Before he joined the Blood Cult."

The photo shows the two young men with their arms around each other, swaggering out of a Perry Street brownstone. Nigel is wearing a white muscle shirt and scruffy shorts. His smile is shy, disarming, his eyes glittery and slitted—a boy either stoned or in love, perhaps both. I wouldn't know—it's been a long time since I had the pleasure of enjoying either state.

To look at him, you would never think this boy had ever hungered—for love or sex or anything else—a day in his charmed life.

Alas, if Nigel's life was "charmed," it was by an evil angel.

For one thing, at the time he was conceived, I was a nineteen-year-old drug-addled hooker. When I wasn't sucking off a john, I was pushing a needle into my arm. I'd already had two abortions and decided to keep this child, not because of any latent maternal instinct that surfaced between the bedroom and the abortion clinic, but because at the time, I thought a baby would help me hold onto the man I suspected was Nigel's father. The scheme was as old as my lover's sudden disappearance was predictable.

"But I love you", I remember crying out, as though merely saying the words would garner reciprocation. I was always in love with someone in those days—I needed to be in love as much as I needed to breathe. Being in love was the ultimate fix—it buffered me against reality and the self-hatred that I carried inside me like a ticking bomb while I used uppers and downers and heroin and the wrong kind of men to murder myself on the installment plan.

I thought if only I could meet the Right Man, he'd wave the magic wand between his legs and take away my pain.

Like the man that Nigel grew up to be, I hungered desperately for love and squandered myself in search of it.

And along the way, I found that answered prayers are often the first step toward damnation.

The summer that Nigel turned nine-years-old, I met The One—the man I'd waited for all my life— beautiful, wealthy, powerful. The man I knew I'd die for. I quit the streets, stopped shooting dope, quit being Nigel's mother. My life was different now. Soon after meeting my new lover, I sent Nigel to live with my widowed sister, a woman as austere and taciturn as I was wild and wanton.

At first I tried to keep track of Nigel through sporadic correspondence with my sister. He was a shy child, I was told, very loving, attentive and eager to please. *He pines for you and keeps asking if he did something wrong to make you send him away*, she wrote. *He keeps asking why you never call or visit.*

But I had other things to keep me occupied by then, and Nigel wasn't one of them.

*How I long for the Master to love me…*Nigel writes. *When I lie beneath the open dome of the Star Room, watching the swirling procession of the planets while the Master's mouth describes its own wondrous constellation of kisses down my belly, when I feel his hardness against between my thighs, I know the meaning of adoration, know that I would give myself to him entirely, commit any crime, endure any torture, if only he might feel for me one fraction of the love I feel for him.*

Oh yes, I understand, son. At your age, I felt the same way, too—that love was a tiny form of death, to be purchased with the heart's blood and paid for with the soul. Not a give and take between two equals, but the conquest of the vulnerable by the mighty, a lush and languid bloodletting, be it emotional or all too literal, of a submissive's life force.

When the Master opens up a cut on me and sucks the oozing wound, I feel a kind of ecstasy. I want to bleed to death for him, to be emptied out, drained dry by my beloved. His beauty makes my eyes ache. His skin has the pallor of paper and seems preternaturally sensitive to touch—I think he feels pleasure more intensely than others. When he kisses me, I know that I would die for him, if death indeed were the price of his affection.

I rest the journal on my lap as the bus plunges through the darkness of the desert. The head of the sleeping woman in the seat in front of me lolls back, frosted strands of hair matted into birds' nests clumps. Across the aisle, a little boy sits wide awake, staring at me in a way that makes me want to scrunch up my face in a monster leer and hiss "Boo!" Instead, I offer him a small go-back-to-sleep smile with a tiny tilt of my eyebrows. He turns away and grinds his spine into the seat back as though hoping it will slide open like a secret passage into some other realm.

I try to sleep, but the twisted, weird silhouettes of the Joshua trees slick with moonglow, the night textured with stars and what might be the leathery winging of bats, the sense of my own mission, make me want to leave my seat and pace the aisle like a penned coyote.

Instead I try to remember everything that my research since Nigel's death has gleaned about "the Master" (nee Edgar Lauren, forty-five years old, former real estate salesman, bit-part actor in some soap operas and a couple of MTV videos, Protestant by birth, sex-god and Creature of the Night by avocation). I've not found much—a few paragraphs on the subject of

Vampire Cults in America Today in *The New York Times*, a page in *People* and an analysis in *Psychology Today* on the phenomenon of people who either pretend to be or actually believe themselves to be vampires. A sidebar interview with an ex-follower describes the Master as seductive, exploitative, an utterly narcissistic combination of vanity and charm. "He drinks human blood, exerts almost hypnotic power over his followers. Is he the *real* thing?" the reporter asks coyly at the end of the interview.

When I read that question, I remember feeling a frisson of horror and titillation. A vampire? My Nigel in thrall to such a creature?

I know that Nigel gave Edgar Lauren not just his body, but his material wealth as well—the trust fund I'd set up for him to receive when he turned twenty-one went entirely into Lauren's coffers.

But then the Master seems to have a talent for seducing those who have more wealth than wisdom, the decadent and trust-funded, the nouveau flush. It's known that the granddaughter of a well-known deceased actor, a man who ironically enough had once played Count Dracula in a stage production, funded the Master's palatial digs outside Vegas a few years ago. Since then, it's rumored the Master never goes outside. The closest he gets to daylight are the facsimiles of skies painted on each of the ceilings in his desert residence.

At times the bloodletting is copious. The dozen or so of us who live here partner each other at random for sex and for the drinking of blood. Only those most fortunate are chosen by the Master. I understand the awful danger in the blood-drinking and yet, I find the sweet, thick taste of blood to be invigorating. It seems to act as an aphrodisiac, but more than that, it fills me when a sense of connectedness, as I take the very essence of the others into my own body.

I read that paragraph several times. If I could cry, then maybe I'd feel cleansed. But my eyes are as dry as the desert scrub sweeping past the edges of the Greyhound's headlights.

Around three a.m., just before the bus reaches Vegas, I open my dinner and eat quietly so as not to disturb the sleeping passengers. I put on fresh lipstick and rouge, run a brush through my silver blonde hair and smooth out the collar of my blue silk blouse. Nigel writes that the Master's favorite color is blue. Sky blue. Like his eyes.

At the rental car company across the street from the bus station, a silver Volvo waits for me. When I tell the girl behind the counter where I'm going, no flicker of amusement or disgust crosses her varnished-looking features. "Skyland?" she says. No problem. This is Vegas, after all, and why shouldn't I be headed for the desert lair of a reclusive salesman turned MTV-extra turned sex cult guru in the wee hours of an August morning?

She draws directions on a map. As I drive through the desert night, I can imagine the fierce heat of midday lancing down, white hot and blinding, but long before the sun breaks like a bloody egg on the horizon and drains into the desert sand, I have arrived at Skyland.

§ § §

The Master says we acquire inner peace through the gift of our material possessions, the gift of our bodies. He accepts material wealth only to relieve his pupils of the desire for acquisition. Our bodies are a kind of tithe. Last night I worshipped him on my knees, suckling like a child, finally swallowing every drop of his gift to me, what he calls the Baptism of Holy Semen.

From the looks of Skyland, I can tell the Master has spared no effort to take onto himself the moral burden of his followers' unholy bank accounts and corrupting stock portfolios. The cult headquarters is an ornate domed castle of pink-orange sandstone, plunked incongruously in the center of the desert moonscape. It's like finding a Faberge egg in the middle of the Kalihari—bizarre in the comic/scary way of a Salvador Dali painting.

To add to the off-kilter mystique, there's a Harley parked next to the door, a Jag and a couple of pick-up trucks that must be used by the Devotees to bring supplies from Vegas. A lighted fountain by the door spews bile-colored water. Borders of stumpy teddy bear cacti that resemble malformed gnomes surround the palace like a profusion of warts.

No twinkle of light seeps from its windowless facade. As I approach the double doors inlaid with Spanish tile, I feel like I am entering the Byzantine necropolis of some corrupt and ancient pasha. It shames me that the feeling is not at all unpleasant. Perhaps it is my own adrenalin-fueled anticipation, but the place seems to reek of sex and blood, hormonal heat. Essences that, even on this most serious of missions, makes desire seethe disturbingly along my spine. A corrupt, pheromonal perfume hangs languidly, like the promise of a rainstorm that will never come, over the premises.

My arrival is expected. A lawyer I acquired in the days when I was amassing my quite considerable fortune has made sure the Master knows who I am—within certain discreet limits—a bored and wealthy eccentric, a one-time callgirl, now in search of erotic thrills cloaked in pseudo-occult gibberish. Although I've been told the Master prefers young boys and girls, it seems greed's given him a hard-on for my more mature affections.

A scrawny, dark-skinned girl with gold rings through lips so plump and crimson they mimic vulval folds greets me at the entrance and ushers me into a waiting area. Simple benches, fringed throw rugs, a profusion of pillows flanked by teakwood griffins decorate the room. As the girl turns to leave, I see the ridged scar tissue along her upper arms and neck, more recent cuts across her back.

I shiver and gaze upward. As I expected, the ceiling is a replica of sky, robin's egg blue, dotted with creampuff clouds and the gauzy, languid haze of heat rising. Track lighting gives the illusion of faint sunlight gilding the edges of the cumuli.

A young man with the pouty mouth of an errant schoolboy and an ugly sore marring the symmetry of his lower lip brings me a glass of tsai. Although I'm hungry, the curdled-milk look of its steamy contents turns my stomach.

While I wait, I continue re-reading Nigel's journal.

Tonight, lying in the Master's bed (while the other Devotees were fiercely envying me, no doubt), I dared to

ask the question I'd been putting off for fear of appear-
ing either ridiculously naive or unforgivably impudent. I
asked if—should we both desire it—he could truly trans-
form me into something more than human, powerful and
immortal. In reply, he used his silver knife to open a gash
at my neck and fondled my cock while he drank from me.

But he still did not answer my question.

§ § §

"Corrinne?"

I hear my name pronounced in syllables sweet
and smooth as clotted cream. My head jerks around as
though tugged by an invisible leash. *The Master.* Time
slows and thickens as in a sluggish dream, as I take
in every lithe, cobra-sleek inch of him. The man that
Nigel loved.

He is as beautiful as I'd expected, yet somehow—
for a man who wields such power over his Devotees—
also more innocuous. No inkling of corruption here—
unless one considers a too-pale and perfect body to
imply some inner evil.

He looks much younger than his age, hair lustrous
and black as enamel against meringue-white skin,
limpid eyes that seek and penetrate while giving away
nothing, forearms ropey with muscle and pelted with
dark, lickable hair.

And hollow. The void in his soul vibrates against
my flesh like a kind of psychic sonar. Perfectly, immac-
ulately empty. Neither saintly nor corrupt, this Master,
but an exquisite masculine vessel in a state of eternal
spiritual, hormonal hunger.

He's dressed differently than what I had imagined. Perhaps I had expected a cape or flowing avatar robes, silk purring around bare toenails, some satin and velvet costume out of a B-grade vampire flic. Instead he's wearing grey sweatpants with a drawstring waist, a plain blue, loose-fitting shirt. But for his extreme pallor, he might be an off-duty lifeguard or a lounging tennis pro.

When he takes my hand, his fingers are unusually dry and cool—as if they've been dipped in paraffin. He asks me a few questions to determine the extent of my interest in and knowledge of his so-called Blood Cult. Apparently my answers satisfy him—or maybe it's the dime-sized emerald on my left hand that convinces him I'm fit to be admitted to the sanctum. He grants me a tour. "You understand what you're getting into? You've read The Work?"

"Many times," I say—pompous diatribe of sex and occult prattle and life-eternal rot that was included among Nigel's things. "It's what influenced me to seek you out." I decide to press my luck a bit. "That, and the fact that I had a son who recently died quite young. His death has given me a new perspective on life's brevity and the importance of sampling pleasure in all its forms."

He still has not released my hand. His sated-predator eyes assess me shamelessly. The way he looks at me, I feel he'd like to fuck me down to sweat and moans, lap the moisture from my cunt, then peel my skin and drape himself inside it, wear me like a robe.

"The other Devotees are occupied with chores," he

says with sudden brusqueness. "Let me see how well you serve me."

I smile up into his empty eyes and too-beautiful face, but it is Nigel's face I see—Nigel's kisses on his lips, Nigel's pain behind his eyes when I answer, "Fair enough. Let me see how well you fuck me."

§ § §

The Master's palatial residence has no windows, but as we move from room to room, shyly spied upon by scarified and pale-cheeked Devotees, I know the sun has risen outside, the earth's commenced to bake, and shadows—red-hot wraiths that mime the phallic lengths of cacti—claw their way like those dying of thirst across the burning sand. Beyond the subtle burr of air conditioners, I'm also aware that heat assails the domed abode and sun-basking lizards flick forked tongues in our direction, as if anticipating a moment when the curved white roof cracks like an egg and sunlight dazzles in.

"Is it true you never see the daylight?"

He grimaces as though the very thought induces goosebumps. "I see no need to leave my residence. I prefer to let my pleasure come to me."

We stroll along a dimly lit corridor where the scent of blood permeates the air like incense in a cathedral. Each time we pass a Devotee, they bow in obeisance.

"There are those who say you stay inside because you have no choice—that sunlight would destroy you."

He allows himself the subtlest smile, but it's clear he's flattered. "Perhaps that's true…or maybe I suffer from some deficiency that makes my eyes acutely sensitive to sun. Maybe I crave blood as a way to compensate for some vitamin deficiency. Isn't that one of the explanations given for the universality of the vampire legend?"

"If it's a legend."

"If you're afraid, you're free to leave here if you like. Later on, I may not be able to make you the same offer."

I take his hand and guide his wrist to my lips, tongue the purple veins wending their way heartward.

"I want to learn all you can teach me."

"About pleasure?"

"And other things."

"Erotic pleasure is the path to higher wisdom." He sounds as if he's reading from a fortune cookie.

Then, perhaps because he realizes his observation sounds facile, he expostulates on his philosophy of salvation through the flesh until we arrive in what he calls the Morning Glory Room, a bedroom whose ceiling offers a pastel facsimile of a dawn sky so delicate it might have been painted on the inside of an eggshell.

His clothing slithers to the carpet like a discarded skin. Beneath it, his body is fetchingly muscular, his alabaster chest the white canvas against which spreads a tree of ebony hair. There's a sureness to the way he moves his muscles—more a swimmer's body than a weightlifter's, more dancer than quarterback.

He slides a hand behind my neck. Undoes my blouse. Cool dry hands, fingerpads like insect husks.

Lust plucks at me like hot, sadistic fingers—heat and hunger supersede all else. How can I so desire the creature I hold responsible for own my son's death?

But I know: because he *was* Nigel's lover and now he will be mine. Because knowledge of his skin, his taste, of the musk wafting up from his pores will bring me as close as I will ever be again to Nigel, the child that I betrayed.

The Master has a little game he plays with me. In private, when he snaps his fingers, I'm to drop to my knees, take his cock in my mouth. Humility and submission are the twin paths to enlightenment, he says. Freedom of the soul through bondage of the flesh and abdication of the will.

As he continues to disrobe me, he turns professorial. "You see, religions have had it all wrong through the centuries. What's denigrated as sexual debauchery is really the path to ecstasy and wisdom. The wisdom of the flesh. Mortify the flesh and bleed it dry. Devote ourselves to the arts of pleasure and pain. Through satiation of the body, we are able to transcend it and find peace."

And your own desert Xanadu and a different lover every night, I think.

He cups my cheek and turns my face to meet his. Something in my eyes, perhaps the fact that they aren't closed, but open, seeing him, *really* seeing him and he *knows* I see him as he is…he hesitates a flicker…then his ego muscles back to take command and he delivers a kiss hot and moist and penetrating enough to unravel the senses. These lips kissed Nigel, I think. This mouth took Nigel's cock into its hot dark and anointed it.

These are my thoughts as I relax and melt into the kiss, let him mold my mouth to whatever shape he wants it.

"You're lucky," he says. "You're special. You have a need greater than most to be...filled in every sense... physically, spiritually...for a long time now your life has been as barren, as devoid of love as the dried up, cracked arroyos splitting the desert."

I neither confirm nor deny this assessment, but lie back on the bed and allow his strumming tongue to play its song between my thighs. Time seems to be passing underwater. There's a slow-motion quality for each movement of his hands, his lips. His caresses are stretched out like slick, moist taffy until we lie so close that the surface of his skin defines the boundaries of mine. I feel appalled at myself for enjoying this travesty of seduction, but the erotic has always had a self-renewing quality for me—it's always new, it always hits with a surprisingly strong jolt of YES, as if a small electrode has been fired in the pleasure center of my brain.

Above me, the pale light illuminates a radiant, mother-of-pearl sky, dewy with captured moisture, streaked with soft curlicue clouds that range out like tassels towards what should be the horizon. The artist is to be congratulated. With my lids half lowered, it looks so real I nestle my head in the crook of the Master's shoulder to shield my eyes from the impending sunrise.

Tonight I took a razor blade and cut the Master's name into my chest. Soon I was white and red as a barber pole. But the Master, when I showed him what I'd done, only looked at me with contempt. I felt appalled, ashamed and filled with a self-loathing that I cannot seem to shake.

I feel myself getting ever weaker, my sense of myself more ephemeral. My will feels as porous and crushable as bones made cracker-thin by osteoporosis.

Adroitly as a Borishnikov of the bedchamber, he maneuvers me through a ballet of sex, never breaking rhythm, never pulling out. It's like a dance, choreographed to perfect erotic rhythm, crescendos of force and near violence followed by long languid adagios of touch so tender it verges on excruciating.

We move to yet another bedroom, accessible from the first one through a connecting door. The bed here is swathed in ivory-colored silk; above it shimmers a fog-shrouded sky where a veiled sun glimmers weakly. I slide down between his legs, bathe his length with my tongue. No blood courses through the blue vein that worms along the shaft, but he stiffens anyway. No surge of blood, but a fuck-you-senseless hard-on just the same.

I run my hand along the shaft, exploring, marveling at what I feel beneath the skin.

"A prosthesis." The irony astounds me. "The guru of a sex cult and you're impotent."

"Hardly impotent." He sounds offended. "Before I had my device implanted, I could get several erections a day—nothing to be ashamed of. Now I can have dozens and satisfy one partner after another. My lovers don't complain."

I decide to tease him a little. "Not to mention the fact that an implant adds to your mystique. A vampire would require such a device, wouldn't he, to get an erection?"

"Possibly. If such a creature existed."

The tang of promised danger wafts off him like a drug. Lust rules me. "I want you to fuck me in every room," I whisper, "underneath each of your skies."

From a drawer made into the headboard of the bed, he takes out a slender silver knife, the handle elaborately carved to resemble male genitalia.

"You know what making love with me involves. May I make the first cut now?"

My gaze travels up the perfect silver shaft, the point glittering like the eviscerating tongue of some Aztec God. I think of spilled blood lapped in coppery tonguefuls. My head turns with wooziness.

"I need more time before I bleed."

"But blood-letting is part of making love here."

"Just a little more time…to get used to the idea."

He stares at me as if he's trying to discipher some secret inscribed behind my eyes. "I'll give you a few days" he says, "but then you'll have to let me cut you." And he puts the knife away.

§ § §

As part of my initiation, I agree to stay in seclusion and be entirely at the Master's service for one week, with each session taking place in another of the many bedrooms. Our love-making familiarizes me with a multitude of skies—one broils with ocher-lined thunderheads while lightning lashes the clouds, another pays homage to dusk—thin tendrils of late sun, a delicate amber kudzu that creeps among clouds so gold-tinged and ethereal that they might harbor angels.

A variety of Devotees—haggard-looking, lily-skinned men and women with downcast eyes that seem at odds with their eerie, suffering little smiles—bring me meals. I have no appetite and, besides, there are other hungers to distract me. Some of the Devotees appeal to me—a blonde girl with breasts like pink-tipped figs and downy pubic curls—I feed her chunks of melon and oranges from my lips and make the many rings that pierce her labia chime like temple bells.

I ask her if she knew a young man named Nigel who hung himself in a domed bedroom that opens up to see the real sky. She listens with sweet solicitude, as though I'm reading her a fairytale, then says she can't remember.

It seems my desirability has diminished as my personal resources have been depleted. The Master has grown bored with me. We have not made love alone in weeks, and when I try to catch his eye, he either ignores me or sends me off on some errand. I'm terrified he's going to ask that I leave, as I have seen him do with others but, in my egotism, never dreamed he would demand of me. The other day, he asked if I had family anywhere. Family? What a cruel joke! I thought I'd found my family within these walls.

More and more I anticipate my time spent with the Master, lust infected with that raptor hunger of rage mixed with arousal—for that flesh that so enraptured Nigel captivates me now, and I bury my face in the sweet curve of his groin, in the meat of his chest and the jut of his jawline, in the musky nest under his arm.

Almost a week after my arrival here, I am finally allowed inside the domed bedroom that I've been waiting to see, the one that Nigel described in his journal, the one in which he chose to die.

A four-postered bed with a satiny purple comforter occupies the center. There is a table with a pitcher of cold water on it and a variety of implements laid out: whips and clamps and various restraints. Metal rings festoon the walls at different levels—a plant in a wicker basket droops from the highest. I don't know if it's a deliberately mirthful touch or if the Master really likes his slavish Devotees to submit to his indignities amid a bit of foliage.

He has requested that I leave tomorrow—the Master, the Father, the man I adore. I've begged and pleaded and threatened to harm myself. He is unmoved. The old demons from my childhood bay at me like rabid hounds— once again, I am abandoned and betrayed by the person most important to me in the world. Once again, I am unworthy. Once again, I am alone.

"This is my favorite room, my special room. Sound-proofed for greater privacy," he tells me as he fondles a leather riding crop that dangles from a hook near the single touch of greenery. "I think I've given you time enough. I want to see you bleed."

"Beneath the stars?"

He nods. "There are those who believe I never see the real sky, but they're wrong."

He presses a button by the bed. The ceiling, which bears a replica of desert day at its most scalding, when the sun is at its zenith, spirals back and the night opens up above our heads like a pinpoint pupil slowly dilating until it fills the entire eye.

As the ceiling opens, so do I. On my back, legs supported by his shoulders, I can see Venus and her entourage pulse and blaze. The star patterns seem to dance, dipping and wheeling like the constellations of pain that flash behind the eyelids after a blow.

"Are you willing to give up all that you possess for me?" the Master says.

"Are you willing to sacrifice all that you have and all that you are and could ever be?

"Are you willing to be one of the Devoted?"

The "yes's" come as easily, as unthinkingly as my climaxes. His tongue feasts on my neck. A bite above my collarbone, a nip beneath my hair. His teeth are gentle. The skin remains unbroken while above my head the stars twirl like drunken Sufis.

"You drink the blood of others," I tell him, "but when do you bleed? Or is it that you like your followers to think you don't bleed at all, because of what you are?"

But then before he can answer, I pull him down to me and make fierce love to him, and this time it is really love we make, for I have always felt a strange, almost euphoria-inducing affection for those whose lives I am about to end.

It is decided—I know how and where that I will die. Tomorrow in the room that is the Master's favorite I will tie a noose around the highest of the hooks and hang myself. I will make sure to do the deed at night, after I open up the dome so that in my last moments, I can see the night sky. The real sky, not another of the Master's painted ceilings.

I wonder where my mother is. I wonder who—if anyone—will tell her what I've done.

Afterward, when we have finished making love, the Master pushes the button by the bed again, replacing the night sky with a false and vivid noon. We lie entwined, him sated, me with nerves as keen as tiny wires, before I straddle him and let him feel my strength. I see the astonishment and then the terror in his eyes—terror not because he thinks I'm going to hurt him but because he's being overpowered by a woman, his masculinity is compromised as his wrists are forced above his head and fixed into the leather bonds that attach to metal clips around the bedposts.

I pat his porcelain cheek and run my finger across the punctures that my kisses have left behind his ear.

"Do you understand that you've become what you pretend to be?"

He gives me his benevolent, mildly chastising smile. Christ looking down from the cross: Forgive them Father, they know not what they do. "I don't believe in vampires."

"But you are a vampire—a human one who sucks the life force from your victims. I think that kind of vampire's more despicable. At least you have a choice."

His lower face cracks in a laugh, which ends abruptly when the heel of my hand smacks his jaw out of allignment.

"The son I lost? His name was Nigel and he killed himself in this room, because you used him and then cast him aside.

"I know how Nigel must have felt. I was obsessed with a beautiful man once, a man I was willing to die for. I *did* die for him, to become like him, just like you're going to die for me."

I bite him hard.

Smile redly.

This time I let him see my fangs.

I lean down to give his wrist a lacerating kiss that penetrates the bones. The sensation of my fangs popping his flesh and sinking down through fat and skeletal system is like an orgasm that explodes in my mouth and travels to the far reaches of my body. Eternal Death flows with my spit. His sweet blood stains my teeth.

He screams for help, and I remind him that the Star Room's walls are sound-proofed.

"It's hard not to finish you off right now. I haven't eaten since a sleeping woman with ratty hair on the bus that brought me to Vegas. I could have had my chauffeur drive me out, but it's nice to snack along the way."

A final, deep drink from his screaming throat: for Nigel.

When I turn the switch to make the painted ceiling spiral open, unveiling the night sky, he begins to struggle, but I've drained too much of his blood by now. Not having fed, he has no strength to break his bonds, so he makes empty promises.

He'll partner me, he'll be my lover, we'll hunt and kill together. A perfect, if unholy, pair.

Perhaps those words are what make me realize more than ever why I can't let his existence continue as one of my Kind. We are so much alike, except he feels no shame, no guilt. His hunger and his evil exceed mine.

I stand on the other side of the door, relishing the agony of his anticipation. Once I peek in and see the inkiness of desert night has faded to the gentler, blue-tinged black preceding dawn. Then I shut the door again, but leave it cracked a hair.

When the desert sun begins to rise and his dead flesh starts to scorch, I hear the savage music of his screams.

Walled

It was just after the twenty-second anniversary of her confinement in Dunlop House Hospital on Glasgow's Carrick Glenn Road that Plush awoke one night and heard the sound of something mewling, trapped inside the wall.

She thought at first it was a young child crying, and, for an instant, it felt as though her heart stuttered to a stop.

She lay there, mesmerized by the sound, which wrenched at her guilt-filled heart with notes as keen and piercing as a shard of bone.

"Forgive me," she whispered, praying it might be Colleen who cried out to her in the darkness.

But no, not a child at all. A cat…

…*inside the wall.*

A dream, she thought, or some kind of auditory hallucination, although, during all her years at Dunlop House, Plush had never been one of those patients who heard otherworldly voices, alien music crooning odes to suicide and mutilation and cantos to atrocity. Her madness, what little had not been leeched out of her by nearly two decades of stultifying confinement, was of a different nature.

When the sound continued, Plush got out of bed and tiptoed to the single window that overlooked the street. Moving about quietly at night was a habit she'd acquired from the years she'd shared a room with light-sleeping Geraldine, whose stroke the month before had resulted in Plush's relocation to a single room in the north wing of the building. She raised the shade and peered out between wrought iron grillwork of a sufficiently rococo design — vines ornamented with spirals and cunning coils — to suggest more artistic whimsy than a method of ensuring that the occupants of Dunlop House stayed caged.

At this hour, the steep and winding Carrick Glenn Road was hushed and nearly empty. Wind-whipped litter rustled along the pavement. A pair of punk-haired women, lipsticked and leather-clad, rocked inebriately in each other's arms outside the lesbian jazz club across the street.

Plush took in every crannied door and ledge, each bare branch of the scrawny elm outside the Take-Away shop a few doors down.

There was no cat.

The sounds of feline distress had not diminished, though, nor was Plush any less clear as to their source.

Muffled by the bricks, but still unmistakable, the cries emanated from the wall behind her bed.

Quietly Plush pushed the twin bed away from the wall. She got down on her hands and knees and crept along the floorboards, searching for some niche or crevice where a cat might hide.

There was no such nook, no acceptably spacious cranny. No place a mouse, much less a cat, could crawl.

And yet the cries persisted.

Plush found herself weeping with despair and help-lessness. The sound reminded her of what she wanted to forget: that she, too, was a prisoner. Whatever the circumstances of the animal inside the wall, she was in no more position to help the wretched creature than she was to free herself.

None-the-less, she put her lips against the cold brick and whispered, "It's all right. Be brave. I'll help you."

§ § §

Although she had been admitted to Dunlop House more than two decades earlier, Plush was certain that she had, in fact, gone mad not prior to, but in the course of her incarceration there.

Madness of monotony and boredom had caught up to her within the very walls of the asylum which purported to be capable of healing her, its claim on her mind increasing exponentially the more closely it was bracketed by the visits of tut-tutting and bespeckled doctors claiming to possess a cure.

But what Plush considered sanity, her doctors regarded as clear proof of its absence and by the time, according to their standards, she was sufficiently dulled and grounded by captivity to pass for sane on their bleak terms, they found her case no longer of sufficient interest to contemplate release.

Neither affluent nor educated and female besides (three conditions that added up to near hopelessness of anyone's taking her plight seriously), Plush was the eldest daughter of a cattle farmer and his wife from Stromness on the island of Orkney off Scotland's northern coast. A peculiar and reclusive child, she was close only with her grandfather Mooney, a fisherman who claimed to have seen a vision of the Virgin Mary while being held in a Japanese prison camp in World War II.

No one gave much credence to Mooney's tale, except for Plush, who'd experienced enough visions of her own to perceive such things as ordinary. She had her own name, in fact, for the dull and limited range of perception most people seemed confined to: the Narrows.

She had few words, however, to describe the miracles that sometimes visited her, but would wander the shore alone for hours beside the glittering North Sea, eyes slitted down to the thinness of incisions, bedazzled by the swirl and glamour of her private universe, the haunted murmuring of the wind, the baleful lamentations of the tides.

And, as an artist paints his or her most secret mindscapes, so Plush's thoughts unfurled like so much blank canvas and let the Universe scrawl across her senses its mysteries and magic, lush secrets that bewitched and titillated and appalling, wondrous doodles of the perverse and blasphemous.

When her sight was at its keenest, she could slip between the sea and sky at the horizon fold where they converged like silken labia and penetrate a realm of arcane geometry, where time unfurled in bends and coils and seasons were spawned, not in straight lines but spirals, the future turning in upon itself to birth the past and present, all three as singularly knit as a single wave that breaks into several smaller ones upon colliding with the shore.

"A simpleton," the neighbors said behind her back. "Touched in the head," muttered her own mother, but Plush knew it was they who lacked for vision, they whose sight was so limited as to be just short of blind.

They saw the Narrows only. She gazed into the whole of time and God's design.

Thus she had thrived, a charmed captive to her private dance, until, when she was fifteen, a squall churned with fatal suddenness across the North Sea, drowning Mooney and half a dozen other fishermen. Grief and loneliness made Plush unwary, heedless. Over the next few months, she sought comfort in the arms of any boy who offered her a moment's consolation, conceived a child by one of them, and was summarily evicted from the house by her mother, who said, "No daughter of mine is going to bear a bastard and raise it in my house."

Plush took a job waiting tables at the Braes Hotel and moved into a small stone cottage near the sea, where she gave birth, a few months later, to a daughter whom she named Colleen. The baby was a comfort and a joy and Plush enjoyed two years of relative tranquility — until the day a woman appeared from Childrens' Aid, acting upon a complaint from Plush's mother who had charged her daughter with being mentally unfit to raise a child and had decided to seek custody.

Plush was distraught, hysterical. She left her job and took to wandering the shore alone, bereft of visions now, beseeching God with panicked prayers to let her keep her daughter.

In the Orkneys, the winter days are eyeblink brief, and darkness never fully concedes its hold upon the land. It was in February, while Plush was meandering along the chilly shore, that Mooney first emerged from the sea to greet her. He wore work pants and an old patched sweater, as if he'd just gotten up from in front of the fire at home, but his form was gossamer and radiant, shot through with smokey light.

"Tell no one that you've seen me, but come back alone and walk with me tomorrow," Mooney said. "Be brave. I'll help you."

And he merged back into the glimmer of the sea.

Plush's ecstasy knew no containment. So much so, that she felt compelled to share it. The next day when she came to the shore, she brought Colleen along. The toddler shrieked and clutched at her mother's hand when she saw the old man's spectral outline separate itself from the sparkle of the water and approach them.

The old man's ghost came forward a few paces and then stopped. His edges seemed to bleed away, sucked into the sea like layers of cotton candy licked by an eager child.

He stared at his daughter and her child, appeared to sigh and backed away.

"Wait! Don't leave!" Plush cried out.

She charged into the sea, dragging the child behind her. The toddler struggled and screamed as the sea spilled over her, knocking her down.

Plush lifted Colleen up and floated the child in front of her. Oblivious to the danger, she waded deeper.

She could see the wraith not more than a few yards ahead now, skimming the pewter water like a low-flying gannet, but more and more of it was fast dissolving, draining into the nearly colorless crease of the horizon.

Tall walls of slate-colored sea crashed over her, cold brine rushing into her throat, numbing her lungs and stopping her breath, and that was when two fishermen who'd been out checking oyster pots grabbed Plush and lifted up Colleen's small lifeless body and took them both to shore.

They had not, of course, seen Mooney. They had only seen a woman battling her way into deep surf, dragging her child face-down through the waves, and they were keen to testify as to the horror of it.

Plush was accused of murder and attempted suicide. Police were summoned, then a battalion of doctors. A trial was held in Inverness on Scotland's mainland. Plush was deemed criminally insane and sent to Glasgow.

Thus she languished for the next two decades in the two-hundred-year old house on Carrick Glenn Road that had served, in the previous century, as a monastery. In such an atmosphere, beset with guilt and boredom, Plush's visions, once her refuge, had seeped away like rare perfume decimated by the stench of offal. The bleak and sterile Narrows had opened up and sucked her down as surely as the cold North Sea had claimed her daughter.

There were no more visions now, no more universe of runes and thralldom, of rotting life and lushly flowering death. Only the stultifying half-life of what others deemed reality and her own burden of self-blame...

...until the night the cat cried out behind the wall and opened up a tiny rent in the fabric of the Narrows.

§ § §

In the mornings, inmates of Dunlop House were encouraged to spend time in the dayroom, a dingy and bespotted parlor where visitations took place. There were splotches on the walls, — the most unsavory of ochres and the grey of clotted sperm — and a heart-shaped stain where a lovestruck schizophrenic had once painted her and her lover's names inside a heart described by her own menstrual blood.

Nearly a fortnight had passed since Plush first heard the cat. The cries were no feebler now than at the outset, though more sporadic, coming at all hour's of the night to torment her waking time and permeate her dreaming.

"Is someone keeping a cat?" she asked Sister Lorna, gazing at the nun's gaunt, pinched face, pale and shiny as a well-licked lollipop. "I thought I heard one yowling yesterday."

She tried to sound as offhand about this as possible, but one does not spend two decades removed from normal society and still retain the skills of artifice and guile.

Sister Lorna made a "you poor benighted dear" face and said, "You know perfectly well there are no animals in here."

Plush tried to look forlorn as she said, "Perhaps I'm only lonely and my ears are playing tricks. I do miss Geraldine so much. I was wondering if I might visit her."

Sister Lorna made a small froggy harrumph, her cue that she felt the request to be an imposition on her already frayed good nature, and said, "Geraldine's still very ill. She might not be ready for visitors. And her face...the stroke she suffered has left Geraldine changed, you understand."

Plush nodded, but her persistence wore Sister Lorna down. Thus, a few days later, a nurse escorted her to Geraldine's bedside in the hospital wing of the asylum, where her former roommate lay with one half of her face apparently in peaceful slumber, the other half contorted in a silent, simian howl.

Plush knew the stroke had destroyed the nerves in one side of Geraldine's face, but she'd been unprepared for the extent of the damage. She'd never dreamed that anything so terrible could befall dear Geraldine who, after all, was a witch, the former Queen of the Lothian Wiccan Order. She had romped skyclad through pagan rituals in her fashionable Edinburgh home and claimed, before she poisoned her drunkard husband into a coma, to converse with the spirits of Aleister Crowley and Saint Magnus. Now she was merely pitiful and old and, until her stroke, had spent most of her time reading the mysteries and history books her children dutifully sent over. Geraldine also functioned as Dunlop House's unofficial librarian. For those who wouldn't read or didn't dare expend the effort for fear of draining minds already sadly overtaxed, she was a source of information, rumor, history.

Now, as Plush stared down at her old friend with frank distress, the woman's good eye popped open and a silver trail of saliva threaded its way out of the corner of the dead half of her mouth.

"Here you go, m'dear."

A nurse brought Geraldine her lunch: a bowl of lentil soup and buttered roll, a small, hard brick of cheese. Geraldine complained that it was difficult for her to eat, what with half her face unworkable, so Plush broke up the bread into tiny bits and spooned green broth into the good side of Geraldine's mouth, wiping her face clean after each spoonful.

"Enough," Geraldine said finally, pushing the food away. She fixed hawkish, deep-set eyes on Plush and mumbled in her slurred, stroke-victim's voice, "Something's wrong. You got that lost dog look."

Plush, already close to tears, blurted out, "The new room that they put me in after you got sick…there's something in there with me…something *alive*."

She was afraid that Geraldine would laugh. Instead, she asked, "Which room is it you're in?"

"First floor," said Plush, "on the corner."

"North wing?"

"Yes."

Geraldine touched a palsied finger to a chin porcine with bristles.

"And would it be…by any chance…a cat that you'd be hearin'?"

At that, Plush's hand trembled so that lentil soup leaked down onto the bed. "How is it that you know?"

Geraldine gave a ragged smile. "Ah, so it's true. There *was* a cat."

110

"What do you mean was? Have you heard it for yourself?"

"Not I, for which I thank sweet Gaia. Just something that I read had happened back when Dunlop House was being built. I had no reason to think it true, but now, with this, the story in the history book would seem to be confirmed."

Plush hated it when her old friend spoke in riddles. "I don't understand."

"Ah," said Geraldine, while the good half of her face smiled and the other half toffee-pulled into something approximating morbid glee, "you weren't aware that Dunlop House was founded on the blood of an innocent creature?"

"What do you...?"

Geraldine shook her grey Medusa locks and grinned a gap-toothed double-double-toil-and-trouble grin. "Don't look so frightened. You've not gone mad. It *is* a cat you're hearin', Plush, sure as day."

"But...we ought to tell someone, oughtn't we? We ought to get it out."

"It's dead, you goose. Been dead two hundred seven years, since this hellhole was first built."

"But how...?"

"Bricking a live cat up inside a wall...it was a fiendish custom that got started in the Middle Ages. The besotted Christian savages thought a cat had supernatural powers, so they'd sacrifice one to ensure good fortune for the building and all who lived or worked there."

"Are you sure?"

"I've read a lot of history books these thirty years since I put strychnine in the old man's haggis," said

Geraldine. "A lot I do forget, but not so terrible a thing as this. A cat was bricked up in the corner of the north wall, to bring good fortune to the Dunlop family and their building."

"All those years," said Plush, appalled. "But I tell you, it's alive. I hear it crying."

"It died two hundred seven years ago," said Geraldine. "What you hear, if you hear anything at all, then it's a ghost."

"I've got to help it."

"It's *dead*," said Geraldine, "Even if its ghost cries out, you leave it be."

§ § §

That night when the mewling started, Plush pushed her bed to one side and put her ear against the wall. A cat, a baby, whatever...the creature was in terrible distress. She listened to the cries and whispered back consolements. Pain called to pain. Plush's skin began to roil. Gooseflesh ebbed and flowed along her arms.

She closed her eyes.

For a moment, she had a glimpse beyond the Narrows, of Colleen's small form being battered by the sea. Colleen's arms were up above her head. Bright water spattered between her fingers like golden needles, but the child's back was turned, and Plush couldn't tell if she were merely romping in the sea or gripped by mortal fear.

Plush pressed her mouth against the wall. "I'll get you out," she whispered.

From her shoe, she took the spoon she'd used for feeding Geraldine and wedged the handle between two bricks, nicking the most minuscule of indentations in the mortar. A few grains of plaster dusted down. She scraped again. The mortar was ancient, crumbly.

Plush pushed the bed back into place, lay down.

Be brave. I'll help you.

It was a start.

§ § §

By the end of the week, Plush's night-long labors had been rewarded with four loosened bricks, all of which she had been able to dislodge and then replace by morning. She'd also swiped a butterknife from the kitchen while the cook was in the loo and kept it hidden, along with Geraldine's spoon, inside one of the sturdy black shoes her sister Belle had sent her for Christmas. The work was tedious and painstaking and many times Plush thought of giving up. But then the cat would cry again, and tears would course along Plush's plump cheeks, and she'd think of Mooney and of the baby daughter she had given to the sea, and how that child must call for her across the Void, and she'd resume her work.

There were no more escapes, however briefly, from the Narrows, until the day when Plush, returning to her room after the evening meal, saw someone had tossed a scarf upon her bed. She reached up for the light switch, then stopped.

The scarf on the bed stirred, uncoiled itself into something vaguely feline, cat-like and yet like no cat, spectral or otherwise, that Plush had ever seen. Its fur, the color of dark marmalade, was intact only in part. Portions of its sketchy anatomy were visible through parchment skin, tissue-paper thin, and when it leaped from bed to floor, Plush saw its head was still un-formed, less cat than lumpen paper mache mask with mouth and cheekbones missing.

"Oh, God," she said and reached out to offer com-fort to the creature.

At once the ill-formed thing froze with alarm and hackled up what hair it had to raise. It bounded round the room in panicked flight, then leaped up and was gone.

Into the wall…

§ § §

"Wake up," said Sister Lorna. "You sleep too much these days." The nun pulled back Plush's window-shades, let mid-morning light spring across the room like yellow tigers. "Be packin' up your things today. You'll be gettin' a new room tomorrow and a room-mate."

Plush rolled over, still half wedded to a dream in which a flock of skeletal gulls, their tiny bones lumi-nous in the moonlight, plucked Colleen's body from the sea and carried it aloft, wheeling and dipping so that the child's head hung down, revealing empty eye sockets nibbled clean by fishes.

The ghost gulls swooped into the bedroom and tore at Sister Lorna's head. Plush blinked hard, and came awake in terror.

"What?"

"I said you'll be gettin' a new roommate."

"But why?"

As though embarrassed to concede that one of Dunlop House's inmates had made an escape of sorts, Sister Lorna lowered her eyes to her spare bosom and said, "Geraldine won't be coming back anymore. She... went home last night."

An image came to Plush: of Geraldine's soul spiraling smaller and smaller like the whorls of a Nautilus shell and of that world outside the Narrows where her visions had once led. Gone now, the gateway closed to her.

"She died."

The translation from euphemism to hard fact irritated Sister Lorna who began to brush away imaginary lint from her starched shoulders with rapid, swatting motions.

"In any case," she said, "we've decided to use the single rooms for short-term stays, those who'll be gettin' out eventually. So we'll be movin' you to a double room tomorrow."

§ § §

Bleak despair dogged Plush throughout the day. That night, the moment that the lights went out, she pushed her bed aside, removed the bricks she'd already loosened, and went to work.

Two-hundred-seven years away, the cat began to yowl. The sound trembled through Plush's nailbeds, shivered through the tiny hairs inside her ears.

She labored at the bricks and prayed and dug with butterknife and spoon and fingernails.

The removal of the four key bricks made easier the weakening of the surrounding ones. By ochre dawn, Plush had opened up a foot wide section of the wall. The floor was covered with a thick layer of plaster, Plush' hands and face dusted with grit.

The cat's wailing sounded so loud now she could not believe no one else heard, that all of Dunlop House was not awakened by the cries.

Plush thrust her hands into the hole she'd dug and reached in as far as she could stretch.

"Where *are* you?"

Her hand brushed something stiff and dry that made her think of desiccated flowers pressed between the pages of a book. She gasped and pulled back, tried again. It yielded slightly to her touch, not brick at all, but...

Carefully she reached both arms inside the wall and loosened and withdrew the object she had labored so hard to unearth — the body of a cat, preserved and mummified by its centuries inside the wall.

Plush turned it gently in her hands and marveled at it, this thing of almost unreal loveliness and horror. Gossamer ears, translucent, flattened to the head, paws perfectly preserved, right down to the nubs of claws where it had tried to dig its way to freedom. The eyes were gone, of course, sucked dry by dehydration. Plush gazed into the black and vacant holes and thought she glimpsed the swirl of stars in unknown cosmos, heard strike the first melodious chords of lost and alien sound...

…and tried without success to follow.

She pulled the wondrous remnant to her chest and rocked it as she used to do Colleen, singing softly. It shivered, almost as if on the verge of awakening beneath her hands. Then its re-exposure to the air proved too much and it crumbled into powder.

A dead thing — less than that, a pile of dust — lifeless as its empty eyes.

"No!" Plush let the dusty fragments sift through her fingers. She put her face into her hands and cried until her sobbing was interrupted by the softest of meows.

She feared she might have fantasized the sound, but looked up anyway.

A cat, translucent calico, its thick fur an undulating tapestry of auburns, was grooming itself on her bed. Preening, corkscrewing its lithe tail in round G-clefs of pleasure. The creature was complete this time, as perfect as it must have been the day the builders of Dunlop House snatched it for its awful fate.

Plush beheld the sight in awe. How long since she had seen a living creature except on the street outside her window.

And yet, not alive at all, of course.

The ghost completed washing one patterned paw, then stretched up in an S-shape, opening its mouth in a stupendous yawn. It leaped down off the bed, caressing Plush's legs, her buttocks, breadmaking in the soft flesh of her belly without leaving indentations.

"Go home," Plush whispered. "You don't belong here any longer. Go."

The cat swished out smokey figure-8's around her

wrists. Its calico design unfurled into a plume of patterned fog, which leaped past Plush…

…into the wall.

"No. Go *home*."

Plush reached out to try to touch the vision one last time - her fingers came back damp. She put her fingers to her mouth and tasted salt and moisture.

The section of the wall that Plush had opened pulsed brightly, appeared to widen. Plush pushed her hand into the rent.

From some other bend in time, she heard the tide and smelled it, the beating of the sea on rocky shores, the tang of brine…

inside the wall

…and felt it roll across her then, the extending ripples of an endless shore, where Mooney and Colleen and Geraldine and a multitude of souls washed up like interwoven strands of some vast and undulating carpet before dispersing back again into the whole.

Plush pushed her head and arms inside the opening in the wall and found herself swept into a flow much fiercer than anything the sea had ever shown her. The current of the dead seized her and pulled her in, swept her up in their chilly torrent. The dead flowed past and through her, tugging at her soul, and she gave in to their entreaties and let her mind sink into the cool dark of their oceanic realm.

"*I'll help you, Mummy,*" Colleen said, approaching her. "*Be brave.*"

§ § §

Walled

When Sister Lorna came to fetch Plush to her new room a few hours later, she found her leaning up against the opened wall, breathing still and strong of heart, but limp and mute, with eyes so blind a light shone directly into them produced no observable reaction. And when they took her to the hospital wing and put her in the bed where Geraldine had died, it was the wraith cat who slipped from behind the wall one final time and padded along the corridors to follow after, not to where they took her body, but into sacred realms of mirth and awe where Plush's empty eyes saw holiness.

Girl Under Glass

Eight-year-old Allison couldn't remember when she had first begun to live behind glass. Maybe she had always lived that way. She didn't feel like part of the world—she was an observer, watching and listening and putting together clues to try to figure out the meanings behind the surface meanings of her mother's words. It required enormous energy and concentration, for each word was designed to obscure as much as it revealed and had to be examined like a buried city, layer by layer, to unearth its secrets and warnings and unspoken demands. Even then she often made mistakes—a tilt of the head went unheeded, a furrowed eyebrow or downturned lip was misperceived, and suddenly she felt frightened and lost in a strange, scary land, knowing that she had guessed wrong and that the mother from the deepest dark, the Witch-Mom who lived behind her mother's eyes, had tricked her yet again.

Maybe her life was a test, Allison thought. Her mother wasn't her mother and her father wasn't her Dad. Her true parents were wise and distant. They watched over her and hated it when she suffered, but it was necessary. They were testing her courage, her ability to endure loneliness and fear. They would come for her some day. They would take her home with them and she would be in a place she belonged. She would be safe and she would be free, and her real mother's face would not change when she least expected it, beautiful one moment, fierce and cannibal-like the next.

Other times it was hard for her to believe there was any world at all except the one she looked at from behind the glass. Her mother's voice, her scary smiles and angry laugh, her needs and silences and secrets, filled up every niche and nook of her life, so much so that sometimes it felt like there was no room left for Allison herself. Sometimes, from the way her mother acted, she got the feeling there really was no Allison— that she was just a smaller, separate piece of Mom.

In order to survive, she became as cautious and attentive as a spy. She watched her mother constantly. Did she seem happy? Angry? Sad? Had she done something wrong? Her Mom would never tell her, she would make her guess. Sometimes she did this by refusing to speak to her at all, reducing Allison to tears and pleading.

But that was bad, too, because tears upset her mother.

"Don't cry, Allison. You make Mommy feel bad when you cry. You make me feel like I'm not a good Mommy. Besides what do you have to cry about? Look at all these toys, all these dolls. What more could you want?"

What more could I want? thought Allison.
Something. Anything. Everything.
Air.

Sometimes it felt like there was less and less air in the world, like her lungs were two tiny raisins. Her mother sucked everything in, all the air, all the light and color and life from the world.

This past week had been especially bad. Her mother had been moody and tearful, not answering the phone, leaving the TV playing night and day while nobody watched. Then, suddenly, for no reason Allison could figure out, everything changed. Her mother's spirits lifted. Now she could hear her upstairs, humming a tune, sounding happy and light-hearted again.

For Allison, it was an opportunity to sneak into the hall closet, where she rummaged around until she found her yellow galoshes underneath some other shoes. From one, she withdrew her most treasured possession—the photograph her father had taken when she visited him in Jacksonville the spring before. The picture showed a plump, red-headed woman in a black tank suit—Daddy's friend Julia—surrounded by four children. Allison was standing next to eight-year-old Andy, while six-year-old Caitlin and three-year-old Pam sat in front. They were sculpting a city out of sand, a long, jumbled creation of squat little houses and straight streets marked out with long strands of purple seaweed.

The beach had been crowded that morning, and Allison wished her father had asked a passerby to take the photo, but she knew he preferred to be on the sidelines, snapping pictures or giving instructions rather than participating himself. Sometimes Allison felt angry at him for not seeing her unhappiness and bringing her to live with him. Sometimes she felt sorry for him—he was so quiet and distant that she suspected he, too, lived behind glass.

"There's really no need to tell your mother about Julia," her father had said. "You understand, don't you?"

Oh, yes. She hated hearing the fear in her father's voice, but she understood. Her mother would be furious if she knew Dad had a girlfriend and that Allison had met her. It was risky even to have kept the picture, but Allison couldn't leave it behind. It was too precious a reminder of a time when she had felt loved and accepted.

"Allison? Allison, come up here. Mommy wants to talk to you."

Quickly, she hid the photo and ran upstairs.

Her mother was in the bedroom, sitting before the mirror, dabbing wine-colored paint out of a little red bottle onto her nails.

"I've come to a decision," she said. "It hasn't been easy, but now that I know what has to be done, I feel like a great load's been lifted. Tomorrow we're going away on a trip."

"Good," said Allison, not sure if it was good or not and more confused than ever. Except for her rare visits to Jacksonville, in her seven years, she'd never been anywhere outside of Rocky Mount, North Carolina. Her mother always said you needed a man to be able to travel and since Allison's father had left them—*cowardly scum*—they were all alone in the world. They didn't go out much because it was too dangerous. They didn't make friends with the people who lived in their row of expensive town homes because *you really can't trust anybody these days*, her mother said.

"What about school?"

"Oh sweetheart, don't fret about school. School's not important. What I've got planned, that's all that matters. And we're going to a beautiful place, a place where I was the happiest I've been in my whole life. I can't wait to show it to you."

Her mother's smile was blazing cherry red, her sly blue eyes sparkly as stars under powder blue lids. The only hint that something was amiss was that she couldn't meet Allison's gaze. She glanced at her reflection in the mirror while she stroked the red paint onto her nails.

"I suppose I should tell you the truth, Allison. You're old enough to know. The reason we're going away—your father has done something terrible."

It was hard for Allison to imagine her father doing anything wrong, let alone terrible—he was always so quiet and cool and perfect that often he seemed barely alive. His eyes were quick and nervous; his voice soft and slow as water dripping from a tap. Allison imagined he planned out every word before he spoke and, even then, he seemed always fearful of saying the wrong thing.

Now, hearing the rage in her mother's voice, she thought of the quiet, nervous father who stood stiff as a child after a spanking. She felt afraid for him.

"Are you going to hurt Daddy?"

"Hurt him?" Bitter lines and an inner darkness twisted her mother's face. "Oh yes, my darling, we're going to hurt him. We're going to bring him to his knees."

§ § §

The next morning, her mother was up early, breezing about in a great flurry, filled with bustle and purpose. Her movements were theatrical and exaggerated. To Allison, she seemed more like a woman in a play pretending to make toast and scramble eggs than a woman at home really doing it.

Allison remained behind the glass wall, watching and listening and trying to figure things out. Her mother took only an overnight bag for both of them and a pair of expensive new dresses she'd recently bought for Allison and herself, still on hangers and wrapped neatly in plastic.

While her mother was fussing with her makeup, Allison took the photo from its hiding place. She slipped it inside the jacket of a book of childrens' stories and carried it out to the car, where she tucked the book underneath the passenger seat. Somehow just knowing it was there made her feel less alone.

When they finally left the house, her mother was quiet at first, her mouth a thin line of red, her eyes fixed furiously on the highway as she clutched the wheel of the Mazda. Then suddenly the words started spilling out, faster and faster, stinging and sharp, like she was vomiting pins.

"I don't want to upset you, but I suppose you ought to know the truth—your father has betrayed us yet again. He's remarrying."

Allison felt a small poof in her glassed-in midsection that might have been pain or surprise or just the result of too much ice cream after dinner the night before.

"It's going to happen tomorrow in the very same church where we were married. Your father didn't even have the decency to tell me. I had to hear about it from friends. That's why I've been so mopey and sad lately. It hurts so much to have even more proof that he doesn't love either of us and never did." She turned to Allison. "That time he invited you to visit him in Jacksonville— that wasn't because he really wanted to see you, you know. He knew it would upset me for you to go away, and your father takes great pleasure in upsetting me."

Allison felt herself getting younger and smaller. Now she was five and her mother was screaming at her because she'd just come from the beauty parlor with a new hairdo and Allison hadn't told her she looked beautiful. Now she was four and her stomach hurt, but she couldn't say anything, because her mother was getting ready to go to a party and the babysitter was late and her mother was getting impatient. *Who does that girl think she is, keeping me waiting like this?*

"I always thought your father would realize how stupid and childish he'd been and come back to me," her mother was saying. "We were happy once. We could have been happy again. I know you don't remember it, but we had a lovely home on a hill when we first moved here to Rocky Mount right after you were born. There were sugar maples and oaks that turned red in the fall. A hammock on the porch and a swing set in the back-yard for when you were older. Sometimes in the early morning or at nightfall foxes would come out of the woods and prowl around the house. Beautiful red and brown foxes with golden eyes, looking for something to kill."

Allison's head hurt when her mother spoke so rapidly, spitting out syllables as though they tasted bad, as though they vaguely disgusted her. She let her mind drift back to the day on the beach when she had felt happy and loved. She wished she could look at the photograph, just to make sure that day had really happened, that it hadn't all been a dream.

"And owls in the trees, big, noble-looking owls sitting up there like judges behind the bench. They'd swoop down on field mice and rip them apart. Often I'd find the remains—little mouse skeletons on the front porch and scattered all over the grass."

She remembered how it had felt to squish the wet sand in her fingers and mash it between her hands. She thought of how Andy had molded the sand into small houses and how Julia had added funny-looking roofs made of grass.

"Sometimes life is cruel," her mother said, "like it was for those field mice. Sometimes we have to do things we don't want to do. Like what we have to do to your father and his little bride."

Her mother veered suddenly out of the right lane into the path of a jeep that was speeding up to pass. The driver blasted his horn. She jerked the wheel and the car skidded back to the right, throwing Allison against the door.

"This woman he's marrying—she's *nobody*, no one at all. A drugstore clerk with three children of her own. Let me tell you something, Allison, I could have had more children. I *wanted* more. It was your father's fault that I didn't. He can't really perform the way a man's supposed to, you know. He can't really make love. It's not something you should have to know about at your age, but the truth is, Allison, his penis doesn't get hard the way it's supposed to and when a man can't get his penis hard, well, he goes a little crazy. Because that's all men really think about, their penises. It's like they don't have hearts, they just have sex organs."

Allison wanted to cover her ears and shut out what her mother was saying. She stared out the window and imagined the sound of the ocean and the heat of the sun on her back. Andy and Pam and Caitlin were laughing and teasing each other while her father stood off to one side snapping pictures, trying to get everyone to stay still.

"Here, we need a church for our town," Julia had said. "Can anybody make a steeple? And how about cars? We can't have a town without cars."

Allison had smooshed handfuls of sand into a pancake and made tiny cars, adding small round shells for the tires.

"Wonderful, Allison!" Julia had said. "This one's a Volvo and this is a Mercedes. These are wonderful cars!"

"Are you even listening, Allison? Sometimes you remind me of your father—I'm talking to you, I'm trying to explain things as best I can—and you just stare off into space—"

"I'm listening, Mom."

"—like some kind of zombie."

§ § §

Around noon they stopped at a Howard Johnson's outside Fayetteville, South Carolina.

"Wait here." said her mother.

"Are you going to get us something to eat?"

"What?"

"I'm hungry. Will you bring me back ice cream?"

"Ice cream? You had ice cream yesterday. You're a little ice cream pig. Sometimes you're so like your father—so selfish and self-absorbed. Sit here and stop whining while I go inside to use the phone."

Allison sat. Her stomach rumbled. She wanted to take the photo out of the book and sneak a peak at it, but she didn't dare. In a few minutes, when her mother came back to the car, she was smiling and tossing her head the way she did when she was trying to get a man to notice her. Her blue eyes were a shade darker, darting back and forth as though she had some terrible secret.

"I called the country club. The wedding's at two. That's good. That will work out perfectly." She took Allison's face in her hands and kissed her forehead, the tip of her nose. She looked almost as happy as she did after one of her shopping trips. "Oh, darling, we're going to make your father's wedding day absolutely unforgettable."

She looked at Allison with a strange and hungry tenderness—as though she couldn't decide whether to hug her or make a meal of her.

"Now, how about ice cream? Don't you want a big double dip ice cream cone?"

Allison wasn't sure anymore what she wanted, but she didn't think it had anything to do with food. Her mother's smiles and good mood scared her. She knew her mother's sudden happiness was dangerous—it could smash all the dishes and cups in the cupboard or rip up all the pages in Allison's coloring book if things didn't go her way and then her mother would insist she wasn't really angry at all—she was actually *happy*, because now she could go and buy new dishes and Allison could have a brand new coloring book—ten coloring books, because *my daughter will have only the best, only the best for my Allison.*

"How come you're letting me eat ice cream again when you just said I couldn't have it?" she asked, thinking that maybe this was a test, that maybe she was supposed to say *No thank you, I don't want any ice cream.*

Her mother's big gleaming eyes swamped with tears. "Because I love you so much, sweetheart."

Allison nodded and said "I love you, too," but the words came out of her mouth like cardboard, flat and feelingless.

§ § §

That evening they stopped in Savannah, Georgia, and checked into a motel. They watched TV together in bed and then Allison fell asleep in her mother's arms.

She woke up in the deep dark of midnight, awakened by some inner warning system that told her that her mother wasn't in the bed. Her mother was looking at herself in the long mirror on the back of the bathroom door. Her fingers were moving slowly, delicately, over her face and body, as though she were a blind woman who'd forgotten who she was. She touched the edges of her eyes, her brows, and traced the line between her plump, soft-looking lips. She lowered her nightgown so that the satiny material slithered to her hips. She caressed her breasts and made little circles around her nipples.

"So beautiful," she whispered.

Allison watched with dread. She knew her mother was asleep, and that some other woman was peering through her mother's eyes, from inside her mother's skin. Something changed in her mother when she walked and talked in the night. Something dangerous and hidden came out that Allison could only guess at, could sense like the shift in an animal's eyes just before it attacks.

The week before, her mother had actually gone outside the house during such an episode, and Allison had followed her, leading her back across the soggy, dew-sodden lawn while her mother spoke to someone in an angry, low voice, saying over and over, *"Something has got to be done about it, something has got to be done..."*

She sensed that if her mother woke too fast, she might forget that there was any difference at all between Allison and herself. She might get that frightening, hungry look and gobble Allison right down and not even notice she was gone, because really there had never really been a child named Allison, only a little girl her mother had imagined.

She got out of bed and tugged on her mother's arm. "Wake up, Mommy. Come back to bed."

Her mother cupped her hands underneath her breasts like she was scooping up great mounds of soft, melting snow. She blinked and looked down at herself and then back at the mirror, where Allison's face was reflected, her mouth a small round "o" in the shadows next to the bed.

"Allison?" She tugged the nightgown up over herself. "Sorry, sweetheart. Did I wake you?"

Allison shook her head. "What were you doing?"

"Oh, just—you know—looking at myself. Dreaming. It wasn't a good dream, though."

"What was it about?"

"Oh, about beauty and what a cheat it is. How it doesn't last. I used to be very beautiful, you know. I used to win beauty pageants when I was in high school and college. All the boys wanted to go out with me." Her voice got very low, so Allison had to strain to hear. "Everyone said I was going to have such a wonderful life. Even the girls who didn't like me, who were jealous of me and hated me, said I'd have a wonderful life."

"You're still beautiful, Mommy."

"Thank you, sweetheart. But I'm older now—I'm not so glamorous anymore and, well, I did put on those pounds when I had you. Men don't want older women anyway. It's a sad fact. Men are very shallow and selfish and they only think of themselves. Like your father—that hateful man. He abandoned us, he broke his promises, he ruined everything. Do you know he always said that he and I'd get back together someday, that he just needed time, but he lied to me, he lied—"

Allison put her arms around her mother's silky neck. "Please don't cry. I know you're much prettier than that other woman Daddy's marrying. You're a hundred times prettier."

Her mother pulled back suddenly and gave Allison a hard, angry look. "Oh, sweetheart, you're so dear to say that when you can't possibly know if she's pretty or not. Here, come back to bed now. Aren't you sleepy?"

Allison shook her head no.

"Then come snuggle next to me." She reached into her suitcase and took something out. "Look here, imagine what I found under the front seat of the car when I was bringing our things in earlier—one of your books. I wonder what could it *possibly* have been doing there? Oh, well, no matter. Would you like me to read you a story?"

Very slowly, keeping her eyes fixed on Allison, her mother opened the book. When the photo fell out, she threw up her hands in a big show of surprise.

"Why, what's *this*?" She studied the picture. "This can't be you, Allison?"

Allison's tongue felt chalky. She whispered, "Yes."

"And who are these people?"

"Just some people I met on the beach when I visited Dad."

"Well, I think there's some mistake, honey. This isn't you. My little girl would never take up with such common-looking strangers. I know she wouldn't. This must be some other little girl. Not *my* Allison."

Allison looked at the floor.

"Am I right?"

Allison nodded.

"So then there's no reason to hang onto this, is there?"

Allison didn't answer.

"*Is* there?"

"No."

"Good. So you won't care if I tear it up?"

Allison didn't look, but she heard the sound of the photo being ripped to pieces. Then her mother went into the bathroom and she heard the toilet flush twice.

When her mother came back into the bedroom, she was smiling, but the smile was funny-shaped and made her mouth look like she had too many teeth. She sat down on the bed next to Allison. "Now then, sweetheart, which story would you like me to read?"

§ § §

Her mother woke Allison early the next day and dressed her in the yellow and white Sunday dress she'd bought for her. She put on her new outfit, too, a beautiful blue dress that clung like kisses to her breasts and belly and made a wonderful rustling sound when she walked.

They didn't eat breakfast, but Allison knew better than to say she was hungry. Instead, they drove straight through to Jacksonville, then left the highway for a two-lane road which took them to an even narrower road where huge moss-laden trees blocked out the sun. They passed trailer parks and campgrounds and finally turned onto a dirt road where a sign read: *Evelyn Donnally Recreation Area.*

Her mother drove up a steep, curving road and parked on a hill overlooking a lake that appeared to Allison to be as big as an ocean. They got out of the car. Voices drifted up. Looking down, she saw a cook-out in progress. A skinny man with a white apron was grilling hamburgers while some kids tossed a frisbee to a black and white dog. A plump, redheaded woman wearing plaid shorts was casting a fishing rod. A man with lumpy white legs napped in the shade.

Her mother paced up and down, silly-looking in her high heels and fancy dress. "This isn't what I expected. Everything's changed. When your father brought me here, it was very private, almost deserted. Hardly anyone even knew about it then."

Allison stared at the picnickers. A strange skin-crawly sensation tingled through her.

"Allison, for God's sake, are you *listening*?"

Down below, if Allison squinted hard, she could imagine that the boy eating the hotdog was Andy, that the woman with the fishing rod could be Julia—they were happy and laughing and playing peek-a-boo with her from behind these other peoples' eyes. Calling to her from the other side of the glass.

"This isn't what I want," snapped her mother. "Come on. We're going to drive around to the other side of the lake."

She snatched Allison's hand and pulled her back toward the car, and they drove around to the west side of the lake. Here a bumpy dirt road lead down to a shoreline where the beach was eroded and narrow, rimmed with high yellow weeds and grey foam. A dilapidated pier teetered out into the water, looking like something made out of bones.

"Now *this* is how I remember it. Quiet, secluded, serene." She turned to Allison. "Do you know this is where your father proposed to me? We went out in a little sailboat, and we made love right in the boat. And afterwards he asked me to marry him. You were conceived on this lake. Your father put you inside my tummy right out there on that water. It was all so exciting. It was the happiest day of my life."

Allison looked at the gleaming grey water and tried to imagine her beautiful mother happy and laughing and content. Whatever had happened here on this lake, she wished she could give that moment back to her. She wished she could fix everything for her mother, make everything right again, the way she sensed her mother really wanted her to do.

"Why couldn't things work out the way I wanted?" her mother said softly. "Why did your father have to ruin everything?"

Her eyes flashed with a strange, agitated excitement as she took Allison's hand. "No one is ever going to love you the way I do, sweetheart. No one will ever care for you and look out for you the way I have. Things have been so hard, raising you all alone, and your father doesn't love me—I see that now. I always thought some day we'd get married again and come back here on our second honeymoon, but—I see now that was just a fantasy. It's not going to come true, and I feel so—so empty and powerless—like I'm just a worthless person."

"I'm sorry, Mommy."

"He doesn't have the right to humiliate me like this. I can't let him get away with it. I just *can't*." She put her hand underneath Allison's chin and lifted her head. "Look at me, sweetie."

Allison couldn't bear to.

"Some things you may not understand, but remember this—"

Her mother turned the key in the ignition. A tremor of relief shimmied up Allison's backbone. *Finally.* They were leaving this place. She didn't like it here beside the too-still lake, listening to her mother's voice trembling with that scary mixture of anger and expectation.

"—I love you, Allison."

She floored the accelerator. The Mazda shot—

"Mommy!"

—forward *onto* the pier and the wooden beams groaned and splintered and—

"What are you—"

—cracked as the pilings—

"—doing? MommystopMommystopsMommy STOPMOMMY—!"

—lurched sideways beneath the weight of the car.

"Mommmeeeeeeee!"

Allison glimpsed a slice of blue sky. Then the car tilted and murky green water splashed and spiraled up a few feet from the windshield. The car teetered half on and half off the edge of the pier before gravity won out and it crashed into the lake. There was a thunderous impact. Her mother screamed. Allison's head banged the dashboard. For a moment, deadly silence swallowed the car. Then Allison heard the sound of water rushing in under the doors and through an inch and a half crack at the top of the passenger side window.

Allison punched the button that opened her mother's seatbelt and grabbed her hand. The driver's side of the car was sinking faster. Her mother's legs were already underwater.

Allison tugged at her mother. "What should I do, Mommy? What'll we do? Help me!"

But the mother she had once loved was gone. The Witch-Mommy, Mommy of the Night, was spitting through clenched teeth and contorted lips "I told you I'd pay you back, you sonofabitch! Happy fucking wedding day, you bastard!"

"Mommeeeee!" Water was filling the footwells, pushing the front of the car lower, Allison was drenched in cold, foul-smelling lake water, full of teeth and needles.

"Mommeeeee!"

Water roared into the car as it shifted, settled, sank, green water turning inky, sloshing up over the dashboard, the steering wheel, even while Allison's mother still raved and cursed the Julia-bitch—"a fucking nobody from nowhere!"

"Mommy, we have to get out! Please, Mommy, move! We have to swim!"

Her mother clutched Allison's hand and cackled and screamed. The scream took up all the space not yet filled by the water. She looked down at Allison—at her and through her and way, way beyond her into some past with no Allison in it, where Allison wasn't her daughter and never had been. Her flat, hate-filled stare made Allison cease to exist. It did more than disown, it obliterated.

Help me, prayed Allison.

She yanked her hand free of her mother's, reached under the water on the passenger side, and started pressing buttons, every one she could find, until the windows began to creak down. Water exploded into the car from all sides.

Allison turned her face up and gulped a last breath of air from a pocket that remained at the roof of the car. She wriggled and kicked and grabbed for the edge of the window, hauled herself through. Then the black water had her, but something else had her, too, something that lifted her up from below to where the water wasn't so dark anymore, to where threads of hazy sun filtered down like a ladder and the world of light and air waited.

She risked a glance upward. Above her, the surface of the lake looked flat and clear as a windowpane ready to crack.

Allison's head broke the surface and the water shattered like glass.

Acknowledgments

"Unspeakable" by Lucy Taylor.
Copyright 2002 by Lucy Taylor.
First published in THE DARKER SIDE:
GENERATIONS OF HORROR,
edited by John Pelan;
Roc.
Reprinted by permission of the author.

"The Family Underwater" by Lucy Taylor.
Copyright 1993 by Lucy Taylor.
First published in CLOSE TO THE BONE,
edited by John Pelan;
Silver Salamander Press.
Reprinted by permission of the author.

"A Hairy Chest, A Big Dick, And A Harley"
by Lucy Taylor.
Copyright 2004 by Lucy Taylor.
First published in THE SILENCE BETWEEN THE
SCREAMS,
edited by Dave Hinchburger;
Overlook Connection Press.
Reprinted by permission of the author.

"Wall of Words" by Lucy Taylor.
Copyright 1994 by Lucy Taylor.
First Published in "Cemetery Dance Magazine," 1994,
edited by Richard Chizmar;
Cemetery Dance Publications.
Reprinted by permission of the author.

Visit Lucy Taylor at:

www.lucytaylor.us

CPSIA information can be obtained at www.ICGtesting.com
Printed in the USA
BVOW012118090712

294713BV00015B/1/P

9 780985 239978